April 1, 2021

TO SOME ABSENT GOD

*For Jared & Tony
from
Roy Paul Madsen*

ROY PAUL MADSEN

Copyright © 2020 Roy Paul Madsen
All rights reserved
First Edition

PAGE PUBLISHING, INC.
Conneaut Lake, PA

First originally published by Page Publishing 2020

ISBN 978-1-6624-0473-3 (pbk)
ISBN 978-1-6624-0475-7 (hc)
ISBN 978-1-6624-0474-0 (digital)

Printed in the United States of America

I wish to express my appreciation to Jo Ann Sandlin for her attentiveness in helping with the completion of this book.

—Roy Paul Madsen

They say you died for Communism, they, who must, *to some absent God,* give the choicest even of the fruits of youth.

—Max Eastman

Preface

As a young sculptor, artist, and writer, I met Max Eastman at the Huntington Hartford Art Colony where we were artist residents. Max was a poet and political writer, and very old when I met him. He liked the sculpture I was creating at that time and commissioned me to sculpt a portrait bust of him. As I worked on Max's likeness each afternoon, he told me about the people he had come to know in the new Soviet Union when he went there to find out the truth about the death of his friend John Reed, the author of *Ten Days That Shook the World.*

During his time in Russia, Max came to know both Joseph Stalin and Stalin's wife, Nadya Alliluyeva, as well as other political figures important at the time. During the course of Max's growing friendship with Nadya, she told him the story of her tumultuous marriage to Stalin. In the beginning, she adored her husband. She told Max she believed at first that Joseph Stalin would become the Abraham Lincoln of the Soviet Union.

In time, she came to hate Stalin because of the starvation of millions in the Ukraine and his brutal policies and actions. The ultimate horror came when Nadya learned that in marrying Stalin, she had married her own father and subsequently had two children by him. Max Eastman asked me to write a book with all he had told me about Nadya and Stalin's life together.

Nadya's story is told here through the perceptions and narrative of Philip Makharov, a writer-historian eventually hired by Nadya to write a biography of Stalin. The horrific results of Stalin's policies turned Nadya against her husband, and eventually, she and Philip fell in love. Philip saw all the sides of Stalin—a man who wrote poetry, loved the arts, showed empathy when listening to a despairing peasant, yet ruthlessly killed anyone who stood in the way of his and Lenin's dream of a Socialist paradise.

Stalin was a poet, and I have introduced each chapter with a very brief poem, which is subsumed in the text as part of the story. These poems portray Stalin's change of character from lover/revolutionary into a paranoid killer.

I hope this book will fulfill my promise to Max Eastman, made many years ago, to write the truth about Nadya Alliluyeva and her life with Joseph Stalin.

1

Orchid of love,
you still pervade my soul
and send roots to the heart
of my heart.
The hours of moonlight
upon your beauty
will always be mine.

—Joseph Stalin

I picked up a straw and wrote into the dirty floor of the cattle car, "Nadya loved Stalin." Then I drew a crudely shaped heart around the two names and wondered why the words were true.

My name is Philip Makharov, writer and historian of the newly formed Soviet Union. I am traveling westward in a railroad car in the custody of two armed Red Guards toward a destiny unknown to me. My left eye is swollen nearly shut, and my mouth mashed to purple by the fist of Joseph Stalin, for the crimes of writing the truth and loving Stalin's wife.

The rhythmic lurch and clang of the railway car did little to cheer me up as I sat, leaning against a side wall, and stared across at the open slit of a side door that would not quite close. The opening let in a stream of air cold enough to crack your teeth and as clear as God's breath, but not fresh enough to sweep away the stench of a railway car left filthy after several loads of cattle and people. I scratched at the stubble of my beard and watched the trees and snow swish by in a timeless image of winter in Russia. They never tell you where you are going.

I dragged the point of the straw under the name of Nadya and stared into memory. I still thought she had the most beautiful profile I had ever seen, with a tall vaulted forehead and the chiseled lips of a classic Greek youth. Her large dark eyes, luminous and beautiful, gave the impression of nearsightedness, as if trying to bring your face closer to hers but failing in that attempt. This gave the feminine perfection of her features a touching and wistful quality.

In a movement swift and impulsive, she planted a kiss on the corner of Stalin's mouth. "Oh, Koba, I am so proud that you are my husband!"

Stalin glanced at me through Asiatic eyes and said, "Please, Nadya. What will my biographer think?" He was uncomfortable.

Nadya darted a glance at me and said, "He will think you are the greatest man of the age."

The greatest man of the age... The man who invented himself.

A booted foot smashed into my reverie and scuffed up the names of Stalin and Nadya and the heart written in dirt and manure. Two soldiers stood there, rifles in hand. A hog of a man growled. "You have been ordered never to write again."

I nodded, relieved not to be struck by a clenched fist or a rifle butt. The slim apparition of Nadya was gone, yet the essence of graceful courtesy and good breeding remained. I stared up at the rifle barrel for a moment and would have taken a bullet in the head to watch her hands move or see her head bend over a tea glass.

"You will never write again," he had said. Stalin, breaker of men, knew that my need to write was as strong as wire and long as life. He had decided that I should be dead until the moment I was killed. In prison, I had begun to write the story of Stalin's wife on stolen squares of tissue paper, with a pencil stub filched from a guard's desk. A surprise search of my cell revealed my literary cache hidden within a straw-filled mattress. The next time I had to move my bowels, the guards stood there and made me wipe my bottom with what I had written.

No matter. They could not wipe away my thoughts and memories of her until they deposited a bullet in my brainpan. My mind would live, picking bones and moving stones, until I ceased to exist. Nadya believed in her Koba until she felt his thumbs upon her throat, and maybe even then. Perhaps never had such a lovely woman—in mind, body, and spirit—committed herself to such a man without seeing the truth, trying until the end to make him the Abraham Lincoln of Russia, savior of the Soviet Union. Such a love should have gone to someone more worthy. Having borrowed her love for a brief, happy time, I know. What became of Joseph Stalin would be history, the task of others. What became of Stalin's wife is this story. Our story.

I stood up to straighten my back and stretch.

"Do you need to piss?" growled a voice from the Hog.

"Do you need drink or food?" squeaked a voice from another uniform.

I glanced briefly in each direction at the guards before saying, "No, just getting kinks out." Since when, I wondered, was a man sentenced to die by Stalin's personal order shipped out in his very own cattle car and given two guards who worried about what went into one end of him or came out the other? Usually, they would just shoot a man or let him die of exposure and lie soaked in his own piss and shit until he expired. This solicitous treatment was at least better than a summary bullet in the base of the skull.

I stretched to arms-length sideways to see whether all my thirty-five-year-old parts were still there and had not fallen off. It was good to know I was still intact, if filthy from being locked up in Lubianka. A prison diet of black bread and water has melted away the slight paunch and posterior that are the hallmark of literary people, leaving me boyishly slender and feeling taller than my six feet in height. With the growth of my beard and tight, curly hair, I needed only the scarf with blue stripes and fringes to complete the stereotypic image of a rabbi. Trotsky is a Jew, and Stalin hates all Jews. I leaned back against the wall and slid down until I was again seated on the floor. I stretched out my legs, crossed my arms, and closed my eyes in reverie to remember Stalin and Nadya.

I was an historian forced by circumstances to make a living as a journalist—not the first time in history this had happened. I became Stalin's biographer through one of God's jokes.

What was not a joke were the poems written by that murdering bastard. Most were insipid drivel, but some were so pure and lyrical that they seemed to come from a child that had known only love or had wanted only love. This from the man of steel.

Nadya embraced Joseph's poems as if they were her own children, and she ascribed to the man the sweetness she found in them. The poems were written to be published in a woman's heart, and as such, they were as precious as life to her. When I first learned of them, she said, "Of course, I cannot let you see them. It would be sacrilege for any eyes but mine to read them. And they are written in Russian, not Georgian," she stressed with a dreamy look in her eyes.

I wondered how poems of beauty could be written in the second language of Stalin, whose speeches in Russian were wooden, dogmatic, and sterile. Georgian was the language of his boyhood, and in that archaic language must anything of beauty be written.

"With all due respect," I had said, "his speeches are recited like a catechism. Poetry seems entirely out of character in someone like Stalin. He seems to me to be such a political animal and a man of steel like his name."

Nadya frowned at me and said, "Poo. If you knew this gentle, loving man as I do, a man who is giving his life to the people and the party, you would not be surprised by the beauty of what he has written."

"May I please read something of what he has written?"

"I told you no. These are for my eyes only."

"I am his biographer. Do you want this biography to be the essence of the man or a propaganda tract? Do you want posterity to read bugle calls and drumbeats or to understand the man who will become the Abraham Lincoln of the Soviet Union?"

"They are too personal," she insisted. "They are love poems written for someone he loves completely and totally—me."

I badgered her tactfully until she was convinced that letting me see his poetry would add to his glory by revealing the artist in the man of steel. Eventually, Nadya allowed me to read one brief poem that she very carefully selected, a troubling poem written in a curiously feminine script:

> Tell me now to go away and never come again, yet I shall dwell in spirit in lives that might have been. Though I cannot follow you nor you return with me, yet we two shall live as one in grieving memory.
>
> Joseph Stalin

What a strange little scribble it was, so cryptic that I puzzled over it until time lifted its veil. Why the note of loss when his darling, lovely wife was beside him? Nadya leaned forward and stared into my eyes as if wanting an interpretation of the poem from me in answer to her own questions. Her shining gypsy eyes so close to mine nearly drove me out of my mind, triggering a kind of madness that made me struggle not to embrace her. Luckily, will triumphed over wish.

The railroad car heaved and clanged to a halt, and the locomotive hissed in the distance. Lovely Nadya vaporized into the stench of manure and numbing cold. The two Red Guards scurried over to me and aimed their rifles at my head… No poetry here.

I said, "I am not going anywhere you do not want me to go."

Hog and Squeaky nodded, and Hog turned to find out what had brought the train to a halt. He yelled in one of the languages of the Soviet Union but was answered in Russian. He grunted and turned back to me, pointing his rifle. For the first time, I noticed his face, his heavy brows, and Asian eyes, like Joseph Stalin.

The soldier did not like to be studied and poked the rifle closer to my forehead. I averted my gaze. Among wild animals, a direct stare is a challenge that might invite attack. Downcast eyes were suitable camouflage for dark thoughts, and they gave the illusion of submission.

Stalin. The steely eyes of the soldier reminded me of Soso Djugashvili, the Georgian revolutionary who had renamed himself Stalin, "man of steel," a first fiction in his self-promotion upward to the pantheon of the gods. I remembered Joseph Stalin as a middling-size man with a sallow face, pockmarked skin, heavy eyebrows, and black hair brushed back *en brosse,* dressed in a military-style tunic with trousers stuffed into soft boots. (Middling size though he might be, he had the hands and feet of a giant). His impersonal stare always reminded me of an officer in some Oriental cavalry regiment. Nevertheless, give the devil his due: Stalin was admired by all Russians as the *krepki krozain,* the strong master, and they liked the feeling that society was in his grip. Memory groped into my earliest research about him.

How strange, I remembered. All the biographical material I had found to seek the essence of Joseph Stalin was devoid of any sense of life. Even the official biography read like the story of someone who had died a hundred years ago, shadowy and insubstantial in their facts. When I wrote the lengthy article about Lenin's life that had first drawn Nadya's attention to me, I could draw on an accumulation of memories from wife, family, and friends to invest him with the colors and textures of life. There were innumerable letters to peruse to get an inner sense of a man of yearning.

With Stalin, I turned up only sterile blanks of propaganda—no insightful and personal letters, no self-revealing biography, no reminiscences from early companions about his boyhood, no anecdotes by his colleagues about his exploits in the revolutionary movement. Stalin's writings of poetry and his passion for art, symphony, film, and ballet were unmentioned. So quietly did he rise to power that he seemed scarcely to have been noticed until he was in the Kremlin.

The rocking of the railroad car was making me drowsy, and now I needed to sleep, not easy to do in a winter of the soul as well as the season.

2

When long silences creep in
on little kitten's feet
and settle down to stay,
let us dust off the sun
and shake out the clouds,
rinse our dreams in rainbows
and depart into different lives,
ending our tomorrows with a smile
for Camelot in April,
when we loved.

—Joseph Stalin

The cattle car heaved with a harrumph-crash! harrumph-crash! harrumph-crash! as the train roller-coasted over tracks that had settled during the spring thaw of permafrost and then refrozen. I rose into the air with each surge upward and then downward with each crash onto the tracks.

The Hog ran over with his rifle and, to my surprise, helped me sit upright, saying, "Are you all right? Are you hurt?"

"I'm all right," I snapped irritably, rubbing the nubbin that was swelling on my forehead. "Can you at least tell me where we are going?"

"Belo-Ostrov."

What irony! The beginning of the beginning of my story of Stalin's wife. Belo-Ostrov is the station at the Finnish border where Lenin had left exile and reentered Russia during the Great War. The Germans had injected him like a deadly bacillus into the weakened body of the motherland to seize control and withdraw Russia from the war. A milling crowd of workers and peasants had greeted him at the dimly lit railroad station, shouting, "Lenin! Lenin! Lenin!" though none of them knew what he looked like until Kamenev pointed him out. Lenin was the famous writer of "Letters from Afar" that had set the Russian proletariat aflame. As Kamenev walked to meet the great leader, he was followed by now forgotten men like Shlyapnikov, Kollontay, and Ilyinichna, but not Stalin—because he was not there.

All official accounts later reported that Stalin was the first to greet Lenin at Finlandia Station. This first-known stitching of his tapestry of lies was later commemorated in a series of paintings showing Lenin descending from the train at Belo-Ostrov, with Stalin standing behind and above on a higher stair. As years passed, Stalin even came to believe he was there and would speak of himself in the third person: "Stalin welcomed Lenin to Russia," he murmured, suffused in false memory. The others who had the good fortune to be there at that time were executed, leaving only Stalin to fantasy that he had been there at Belo-Ostrov at the beginning of the revolution.

I came to know Lenin near the end of his life, after he was felled by a stroke, and at the beginning of Stalin's rise to power. I had been given an assignment to write an article about him for *Pravda,* which means "truth."

Lenin's appearance surprised me as I approached him for the interview. He was a stocky figure seeming even shorter in the wheelchair, with a large head set down in his shoulders, bald and knobby, with squinty eyes, blunt nose, wide mouth, and aggressive chin. Lenin was a leader through the power of his intellect: detached, rational, incisive, and uncompromising. He lacked colorful or romantic mannerisms yet had the power to explain profound ideas in everyman's terms. This pathetic invalid, this wreck of a once-powerful man, was loved and worshipped as few leaders in history had been. Lenin, swathed in blankets, gripped the arms of his wheelchair as he watched my approach in the cold winter sun with little winking eyes.

I said, "I am Philip Makharov, a journalist come to interview you for an article in *Pravda."*

He squinted up shrewdly. "About what?"

An awkward question. I mumbled, "About the succession of power in the party."

"After I am dead?" He smiled slyly.

"Well...I wouldn't put it way, but—yes."

"My compliments... Timing is everything in important matters."

Lenin was diminished in spirit and vitality from the ascetic firebrand he had been. He was really not up to being interviewed but, knowing it would be published in *Pravda,* could not resist rising to polemics and propaganda. With the Soviet Union at the threshold of being the first ideal state, he launched into his favorite theme: the proletariat must renounce their freedom and submit wholly to the party. Then and only then—in abject surrender—would they be happy. And so on and on and on. I found him to be the kind of intellectual who loves humanity but could not endure people. In Lenin's bones was a supreme contempt for breathing human flesh. I heard him out and then murmured, "What are your decisions on the succession of power?"

Lenin got down to business. "Joseph Stalin is my choice for general secretary of the Central Committee. He is hardworking and wonderfully competent. He is more like a German than a Georgian in his ability to get things done, and he is not overburdened with scruples." Lenin's voice stumbled through a chuckle at his private joke. "He has been only commissar of nationalities, but he cuts through problems like a hot knife through butter. See to it that Stalin's appointment is announced in *Pravda.*"

"Done," I said. "And what of Leon Trotsky?"

"Deputy chairman of the Council of People's Commissars," he intoned grandly.

"Heir to the throne," I murmured.

"The Jew deserves it. Under his leadership, the Red Army defeated the whites and the Europeans and, by God, outwitted the Americans at Archangel. The Yankees make me nervous. Europeans will quietly play their cards with cunning, but the Americans often intervene and fight for reasons that make no sense to any other nationality. A strange people. Trotsky handled everything skillfully and got the Americans to leave. Had he bungled it, we might have faced millions of them to who knows what end. My succession belongs to him by right."

Lenin's reward to Trotsky was sumptuous, and I duly noted it for the article. Trotsky, however, was a Jew, deeply sensitive to his Jewishness, and would be aware that appointing a Jew to rule over a nation in which Jews had resisted assimilation into the population was a dangerous thing to do. It meant nothing less than turning the fury of an impoverished and frustrated people against a helpless minority. The Jews of Russia had fought for the motherland, paid their taxes, contributed to the nation's culture, but remained the eternal scapegoats. The word *pogrom* means "attack the Jews." This was the Russia that confronted the Jews, and Lenin had passed the scepter of power over the *Rus* to Leon Trotsky, a Jew.

Something of the old fire flashed in Lenin's eyes, and he shot me an armor-piercing look. He asked quietly, with third-person formality, "May Comrade Lenin entrust Comrade Makharov with an important matter of state—to be carried out in confidence?"

I was shocked and looked it, but said, "Of course. I am honored." I almost saluted.

"You have an honest look about you."

"Thank you," I said, wondering what was up.

Lenin said wryly, "I am head of the Soviet state but so infirm after my recent stroke that I am under the control of those who care for me. I have reason to believe that many of my orders are not carried out when they conflict with the ambitions of those who have another agenda. My death is not far away, and everyone is maneuvering to succeed me in power. I want to be sure that my last will and testament reaches Leon Trotsky, with a request that he read it at the first Congress of Soviets after my passing. Can I entrust you to bring them secretly to him and bring me back his reply?" He looked at me out of weakness and almost begged, "You may be my only chance to have my wishes carried out. Can I really trust you?"

"Of course!" I swelled with importance and felt myself a part of history.

Lenin glanced at the house and then said, "Come close and tuck the blankets around me."

I stepped forward and wrapped wool coverlets about him.

Lenin leaned forward to let me smooth them out behind his back, and as I did so, he slipped a document into my coat, which I then put into an inside pocket. He murmured, "Bring me Trotsky's answer when you return." He smiled sweetly. "And ask Leon Trotsky to bring us a brace of ducks for dinner in the spring." Lenin suddenly shrank within his shroud of blankets.

"Are you all right?"

"Don't know," he murmured. He nodded toward the house and said, "Nadya...one of my caretakers. Call her to me, if you would."

I first scurried and then ran to the house where a door opened just as I reached for the knob. The face of a dark-haired young woman appeared in a flash of beauty that left me speechless.

She asked, "Is he worse?"

I nodded, embracing her with my eyes.

She turned to scoop up a bottle and a spoon and raced out to the enfeebled giant. She moved like a gazelle under her coat, and I was enchanted by her slender grace. I followed after at a brisk shuffle and savored her elegance as she spooned medication into his drooping mouth. By the time I stood beside him, Lenin had recovered some vigor and nodded appreciatively.

Lenin looked at me and then at her, introducing us with his eyes. "This is Nadya Alliluyeva. She is Stalin's wife." He frowned a little as he glanced at me and seemed to grope for my name.

"I am Philip Makharov, a writer. I am interviewing Comrade Lenin for an article in *Pravda*."

Nadya stepped forward in the forthright way of revolutionary women to shake hands and looked at me with interested eyes. She smiled a little and said, "My husband, Joseph Stalin, is editor of *Pravda*. Why haven't I heard of Philip Makharov? He has spoken of most of his writers, and I do not remember your name."

"This is my first assignment."

"How like Joseph to start you out on a demanding assignment."

"Yes, yes." I smiled nervously. Something in her voice frightened me. This was my first paying job in months, and I could not afford to lose it. Writers are toilet bowls for the mighty.

A cloud passed over the meager sun, and a chill settled over them.

Lenin shivered, devolving in the cold, almost into a dwarf.

"Shall I take you inside?" she asked attentively.

Lenin nodded, drawing his blankets more tightly about himself. Nadya was turning the wheelchair toward the house when he raised his hand for her to stop.

"Comrade Makharov," he said, "you will wish to finish the article together with me to be sure there are the correct nuances of meaning. Please bring me a first draft for review," he said but did not mention bringing Trotsky's reply.

Gavno! I hate having a subject retain control of what I write. Perhaps it was only a subterfuge to bring back Trotsky's reply. And what was that weird request for a brace of ducks?

Lenin snapped, "You will bring it to me, won't you?" Sick or not, the request had the honed edge of command—an order from the leader of the new Soviet Union.

"Of course," I flustered. Why am I always afraid?

"Nadya, would you please be my liaison with Comrade Makharov and review the article before submitting it to me?" Lenin sank deeper into the wheelchair and looked ominously sick.

"Gladly," she said, shooting me a heart-stopping smile. "Please wait here while I take Comrade Lenin inside and prepare him for a rest. We can make the arrangements when I return." She pushed the wheelchair up the path to the house with only the top of the head showing of an old and very sick man. Time was running out for Lenin, and he knew it.

Watching Nadya push the wheelchair was a treat. She took long strides that flaunted her sylphlike shape and walked with such feminine grace that I could only stand and admire. What had Stalin done to deserve such a lovely wife?

The wait was much longer than I expected. When the winter sun sank below the horizon, I felt as if I were sinking into permafrost.

The numbing began in my feet and was up to my knees by the time she returned an hour or more later. Then Comrade Alliluyeva smiled at me, and the chill disappeared.

"When can you complete the first draft of the article?" she asked.

"When I get it done," I grumped. I hate the pressure of time.

Her eyes turned cold. "Don't be insolent. Comrade Lenin is a dying man... How long?"

"A week, more or less."

"Then you may as well write an obituary," she snapped. "This is Monday. Let's make it Wednesday."

"That's impossible," I blurted. "That would give me one day to write it and one day to bring it here. I am not laying bricks." And there was the business with Leon Trotsky, which would also take time.

"Thursday, then. In the early afternoon."

"I can't do it," I bristled.

"Very well. I will inform my husband that you cannot do it, and he can assign another writer."

"I'll do it!" I barked, now alarmed. She has a rock for a heart. She could go to bed with her husband tonight, love him into ecstasy, and have me fired in the morning. I nodded sheepishly before her level gaze and wondered how Stalin could put up with such a demanding bitch.

"One thirty on Thursday, time sharp," she said on a note of command. "If you cannot work under pressure, you need to reconsider your line of work." Comrade Alliluyeva turned and walked toward the house with an imperious stride. She knew she was Stalin's wife.

Desperation seized me. These were frightful times, and I dared not lose this job. Crippled veterans were foraging in refuse cans. Widows and single mothers were prostituting themselves to support their children, lifting their skirts to any man to make a few *rubles* for bread and meat. Trucks were used to collect the starved bodies of those who had frozen in the night, tossed in like so many bags of garbage. Orphaned children roamed the streets like packs of wolves, robbing those alone and vulnerable. If I lose this assignment, I might end up like others in the gutter.

Meeting that deadline was a nightmare. Nevertheless, I wrote down Lenin's declaration of intent as if it were Holy Writ. Literary whore that I was, I praised the intellectual brilliance and courage of Leon Trotsky without ever meeting him. I praised the efficiency and administrative skills of Joseph Stalin without knowing if it was true. I praised the wisdom of Lenin for bequeathing supreme power to get things done to those who could get things done. I praised everyone I mentioned by name through fear in my bones that in these revolutionary times, it was dangerous not to praise everyone if I wished to live through the awful turmoil. Be nice to people on your way up because you may run into them on your way down. And I covered my writer's ass by carefully attributing all praise of Trotsky to Lenin.

By the time the first draft was finished, it was Thursday morning, and it was time to meet with Comrade Alliluyeva and Lenin. The mission to Trotsky would have to wait.

3

> The glint in a raven's eye
> could not stifle a sigh
> for your passing
> into a love gone by.
>
> —Joseph Stalin

I gathered up the manuscript and went down to the street to find transportation to Lenin's home in Gorki. Bitter cold stung my face and made my eyes water as I stepped out the door to the street. Blinking away tears raised by the winter wind, I realized that a car had pulled up before me and waited at the curb with its motor running.

The driver flashed a gap-toothed smile out the window and asked, "Comrade Makharov?"

"Yes," I murmured, surprised.

The driver leaped out of the car and opened the rear door for me. He was small like a weasel and looked both frail and tough, with the pale and pinched face of someone who lived too little on food and too long on stress.

The driver saw my quizzical expression and said, "This car was sent to pick you up on order of Comrade Nadezhda Alliluyeva, who wishes you to arrive at one thirty in Gorki."

"Time sharp?"

"Time sharp."

"And you are?" I asked.

"Comrade Victor," he said, not volunteering his last name.

"May I ride in front with you, Comrade Victor. Sitting in the back seat makes one feel like a chauffeured capitalist."

"How political," Victor said with a laugh and a cough. He slammed the rear door shut and clambered into the front seat behind the wheel, while I went around and squeezed in on the passenger side.

The clout of Stalin's wife was obvious. She was *vlasti*—a person of power who could order things done. As Lenin's aide and caretaker, she could probably get whatever she reasonably asked for. She wanted me to arrive on time and sent a car to be sure I arrived on time in Gorki.

Moscow is gray and dismal in the winter when there had not been enough snow to make the city and trees seem trimmed in white lace, and I drifted into driving reverie. Lenin would be annoyed that I had not had time to bring his last will and testament to Trotsky and receive his answer. A draft of the article was the best I could manage in the time I had. After all, Lenin's last papers were important only in the event of Lenin's death. I could feel his documents strapped around my right calf, under the sock and boot. Only an idiot would have left them around somewhere to be found by an agent ransacking one's belongings. I may be a liar and coward, but I was not a fool. The pressure of Lenin's documents was somehow comforting, and it made me feel as if I were part of a turning point in history.

When we pulled into the driveway of Lenin's *dacha* in Gorki, I was surprised to find two people standing there, in the cold, blocking the way: Comrade Alliluyeva, looking lovely and crisply Communist in a fur-collared greatcoat; and a middling-size man with black hair and moustache with enormous hands and feet, whom I recognized as the editor of *Pravda*—Joseph Stalin. Comrade Alliluyeva was holding a small package wrapped in brown paper.

Comrade Victor stopped the car, and we clambered out. I felt in my pockets for a few kopecks for him until a stem voice said, "Giving tips is an insult to the proletariat of the Soviet Union!"

I froze in midgesture and nodded to Stalin. His face bore the look of *machaltsvo*, a man you do not want to cross, and I felt apprehensive.

I sensed the disappointment in Victor. A tip looked good to him in hard times.

Comrade Alliluyeva said, "This is my husband, Joseph Stalin."

Stalin said abruptly, "We have seen each other at *Pravda*."

A tweak of jealousy pinched me as she hovered about her husband, eager that he be pleased.

We shook hands, and I smiled eagerly, but Stalin did not smile. He was all business.

"Show me the article you have written," Stalin commanded.

I wilted inside, knowing that Lenin had placed Stalin lower than Trotsky in succession.

"The article in its present form," I smiled weakly, "is for the eyes of Lenin only."

She flared. "Give the article to Comrade Stalin! After all, he is editor in chief of *Pravda* and your superior! It needs his approval to be published!"

I thrust it into his hands, feeling like a fool, hoping I had not jeopardized my job.

Stalin opened the manuscript and began to read it, moving each page to the bottom as he finished it. He murmured, "You write extremely well." When he reached the page dealing with Trotsky's appointment, he stopped, then reread it, his face suffusing a deep crimson. His hands shook slightly, and he rumbled, "Who else has seen this article?"

"Only you."

"Have you told anyone else of its contents?"

"No, Comrade Stalin," I answered uneasily.

"You are not to tell anyone about this article or its contents until I say so, do you understand?"

"Yes, Comrade Stalin," I said, feeling myself walking along the sharp edge of a knife.

Stalin appraised me through Asiatic eyes. "I hope you realize that it is in your own interests that I be able to trust you. I am not a forgiving person."

I felt the undercurrent of menace and almost quivered. I nodded with a weak smile.

Stalin smiled, too, at the edges of his mouth. He had taken the measure of this writer and found me a supple coward.

Then Stalin's face opened into goodwill. "You write extremely well—even brilliantly. This article is thoughtful, insightful, and skillfully written. You have a future with us."

I glowed. Praise from Caesar is praise indeed. Better yet—an income!

Stalin contemplated me soberly. "There will be a great political struggle for the future of the Soviet Union, and your writing reveals that your heart is in the right place. Will you support me in creating Socialism in one country?"

"Absolutely!" I blurted, relieved to still have an income. "I'm on your side, Comrade Stalin."

"That's good to know," he said, then paused, studying my eyes. "We have a problem. Comrade Alliluyeva has not been able to find Lenin's will and testament, which contains the same content as this article. Would you know where they might be?"

I flattened my expression into blank innocence and turned up my hands. "I have no idea," I lied, feeling them strapped around my calf.

She said, "Did you leave them in your room?"

"No," I said honestly.

She insisted, "Lenin slipped something to you. I saw it from up there in the house."

"It was a page of my notes," I lied. "He wanted to see them."

Stalin said, after a long appraising moment, "I will take the article with me to publish in *Pravda* at the appropriate time. You will remember not to discuss the contents with anyone."

I nodded, but added, "It may need revisions.

Stalin smiled a publisher-to-writer smile, "Everything written needs revisions, and nothing would ever get published without editing. I will edit the article personally and publish it at the appropriate time." Stalin turned to his wife and said, "This man has a functioning brain. We must find work for him to do—for us."

The shower of praise and good news was shocking. I could scarcely believe the good luck that had come not a moment too soon.

Comrade Alliluyeva sent a confidential smile and looked at me with approving eyes.

I had passed muster, and an invisible sigh of relief flooded me.

She stepped forward with her small package and presented it to me. "A gift from Comrade Stalin and me."

"What is it?" I asked.

"A sausage."

"Migod! How wonderful! I have eaten nothing but bread and fat drippings for months!"

Stalin shimmered a smile. "There will be more, and better, if all goes well."

"Thank you! Thank you, comrades!" I salivated at the thought of again tasting real meat.

A distant voice rang out from the direction of the house. "Nadya! Nadya! He has had another stroke!" A middle-aged woman with hair slicked back ran into view and grabbed Alliluyeva's arm. "You must come! He's unconscious and falling from the chair, and I cannot lift him alone. You must help me!"

Then the woman noticed Stalin and shouted, "I told you never to come here again!"

Stalin bowed politely and murmured her full name: "Nadezhda Konstantinovna Krupskaya."

Krupskaya shouted, "YOU STOLE LENIN'S WILL AND TESTAMENT—YOU THIEF!"

"I did no such thing," Stalin said emphatically.

Comrade Alliluyeva placed her arm about Krupskaya's shoulders and drew her toward the house, urging, "We must help Comrade Lenin immediately!"

Krupskaya began to run toward the house while glancing back at Stalin. She shouted, "THIEF!"

Stalin shook his head as he looked after the two running women. "I did not take Lenin's will," he announced honestly.

"I am sure you did not," I said, feeling the offending documents strapped around my leg.

Stalin turned to Victor and me. "Comrade Victor will return you to your apartment. Later, we will get in touch with you to begin work in earnest."

"Thank you," I smiled, hoping it was not just talk. Then I noticed Victor. He stared at the packaged sausage with sad eyes of an aging hunchback. He and I clambered into the car. I turned to wave goodbye to Joseph Stalin, but he was again reading the part about Trotsky in the manuscript. He looked grim and dangerous.

We drove in silence for a while and then Victor said, "What do you have strapped about your right calf—Lenin's will and testament?"

"What are you talking about?" I gasped, alarmed.

Victor leaned over as he drove and, with his right hand, flicked up the trouser and pulled down the stocking edge. White papers gleamed. "I saw it on the way out," he said matter-of-factly.

We rode in a speechless void for a time, and then I took out a small pocketknife from my coat, opened it, and carefully cut the sausage in half.

"Comrades should share," I said, handing half the meat to him.

Victor grimaced a smile of thanks and slipped the jewel of meat into a pocket of his coat, saying, "I appreciate this, comrade. I cannot remember when I last tasted sausage"

I did not mind giving precious meat to him. After a day of lies, deceit, and literary cowardice, sharing food made me feel like a human being again. After all, there was no overt attempt at blackmail. In these times, though, anyone who did not play the game with others could find a terrible end. Giving was an implied promise that there may be more and a kind of insurance against the temptation to inform on me. The fact that the driver did not announce to them that I had something up my trouser tended to suggest he was not an agent in the employ of Stalin.

I asked, "Why didn't you expose me back there?"

"You were going to give me some *kopecks*. You were kind."

"One must be human," I said.

"There isn't much of that around these days," Victor said, "and there will be less of it in the future." He glanced at me sideways and said, "I saw how they treated you and how you responded. You are going to be a winner. Can I come along and win a little too?" He smiled apologetically. "I am *malenky chelovek*, a little man."

I answered, "Stalin said there will be more and better. If there is, we will share it for as long as we are working together... I will sometimes need a driver and a friend."

"I will be both," Victor said.

As we pulled up to the curb before my apartment, I asked, "Do you know where to find Leon Trotsky?"

"Yes, I can find Trotsky when the time comes."

"Good," I said and got out of the car. I waved him off with a smile, and he waved back. Then I unlocked the front door to the building and walked to my apartment with a growing sense that my miserable life was about to change for the better. It was too soon to hope, but nevertheless, I hoped anyway to rise above the barrenness of my present existence.

I opened the door to the two rooms of my world, small and paint-peeling but rich in the things that matter to me. In the center of the room was a desk made of a board suspended between two wood crates and held in place by a stack of books on each side. Some of the happiest hours of my life had been spent seated on the only chair in the room, writing longhand on the board that was my desk. In the center of the desk, in the place of honor, was a bound copy of my first history book—*The Bloody Sunday of 1905*—published to good reviews and few sales. The reviews were well thumbed and used to renew my faith in my talent.

The walls were lined with books, some of them on the shelves of the sole library case in the room, the others stacked vertically on the floor. Several boxes of papers resided under a window facing into a brick wall next door. There was no need to curtain the window.

The second room contained a double bed that had not squeaked under a woman in a long time. Adjacent was a small bathroom containing a toilet, a washbasin, a tub, and the coldest water in the world. The mirror over the washbasin revealed that I nearly always needed a shave and a haircut. I did not like to look in the mirror because I see eyes that were black glowing coals and was put off by the formidable expression. On the other hand, ebony eyes set in pallid white skin and curly copper-colored hair did make my image resemble that of a Viking, though, God knows, I was too cowardly to wield a battle-ax.

Bachelor though I was, I was quite fastidious about things like clean sheets and swept rooms. I would not live like an animal who wallowed in his own filth. I swept up and cleaned up and tidied up and straightened up to give my quarters something resembling austere beauty. My clothing was the very essence of threadbare gentility: poor but clean and civilized.

A bare bulb hung down in my study and in my bedroom, but the power was off more than it was on. Candles were the answer and were placed, with matches, wherever I might be when the lights turned off. I fumbled expertly in the darkness and found matches like the blind reading braille. Sometimes, in the evening, I lit candles and placed them about for aesthetic effect and sat down to enjoy barrenness transformed into beauty. Like most writers, I was odd in little ways.

I walked with some satisfaction through my humble abode, more willing to admit that it was not so bad now that I seemed to have the first fruits of success. But then I noticed something. The boxes of writings under the window were not in the sequence in which I had placed them. I walked over and moved them to where they belonged. Then I noticed that they were smeared inside the box and not stacked crisp and neat and square as I always did. Even my thesis box, repository of my hopes and dreams, was rummaged through. Treasured lecture notes were out of order, notes I had hoped to use in classes as a university professor before my world came crashing to an end in the revolution.

Someone had gone through my belongings, probably looking for Lenin's will and testament, which by now seemed to be part of my leg. I did not give a damn. All I wanted now was to keep my job and escape from the dark-brown taste of poverty.

At the same time, I felt the strange formation of resolution and will that I would somehow, someway, keep my promise to Lenin without losing my place with Stalin—and Stalin's wife. I was moved to light several candles and turn off the electric lights. I sat down at my desk and conjured up the face of Comrade Alliluyeva. I wished I had a good cigar and a glass of lemon vodka.

4

I promise you,
who thrust your hands into soil
and turn the land in strife,
I will ease your killing toil
and lift your eyes to Life.

—Joseph Stalin

Stalin's wife was right. My article would have been an obituary. That night, Lenin had another stroke, and then another and another, and he died. He worked until the end with the strength he had left and had given his last command to me: speak to Leon Trotsky.

Torrents of despair flooded across all Russia, cries that this *Rodnoi Otets*, "Our Father in the Flesh," must never be consigned to the earth like other mortals. Only the funeral of a Tsar, the original *Rodnoi Otets*, could equal in anguish the outpouring of grief at the death of Lenin. Trains filled with workers and peasants—Uighurs, Tatars, Kazakhs—poured into Moscow to attend Lenin's funeral. Hundreds of thousands of people filled the streets to catch a glimpse of the man who had filled their wretched lives with hope.

Then the dark *Rus* began to do what he had forbidden them to do—transform him into a God. Plans were made immediately to commission statues to confront everyone over six time zones; books were assigned that praised him to the sky and put him in a pantheon with Marx and Engels; and artists were contacted to begin paintings that would glorify every aspect of his life. How Lenin would have loathed all this. Whatever else one might say about him, Lenin was modest. The only monument he had wanted was a functioning Socialist state.

My credentials as a writer for *Pravda* got me through the teeming crowds to a good viewpoint at Lenin's funeral. I saw at a glance that the event was entirely out of keeping with the unassuming character of Lenin, whose contempt for pomp and ceremony was legendary. His casket lay in state in the House of Trade Unions amid a mountain of red flowers and banners.

Word was out that Stalin had ordered a stone mausoleum constructed in Red Square for the permanent display of Lenin's body, despite the protests of Lenin's widow, Krupskaya and the indignation of Bolshevik intellectuals who knew that Lenin would be outraged.

I realized, however, that Stalin understood the religious instincts of this peasant nation. Lenin's tomb was to become a place of worship and pilgrimage, the focus of a new messianic faith. Leninism would supplant other faiths with a new prophet in his holy sepulchre. Socialism would assume the forms of a religion, its canons a blend of *The Communist Manifesto* and the Orthodox prayer book. Just as early Christianity assimilated elements of pagan rites and beliefs and blended them into its own concepts, so now the new Socialist order would absorb elements of the medieval past and display them as the trappings of Socialism.

It seemed obvious that Stalin must know that all this ostentation was a mockery of the real Lenin, but he understood his people. A ceremony then began to inculcate a primitive semi-Asiatic nation with a sense of exaltation for the new cult of Leninism.

Lenin's widow, Nadezhda Konstantinovna Krupskaya, sat on a chair to one side of the bier, hands in lap and eyes staring in shock at her late husband.

Contenders jockeying for power stood around the bier, and it was possible to detect who was who in their relative positions about the casket. Joseph Stalin was first among equals and stood at the head of the bier. Second among equals were Grigory Zinoviev, a former actor who could say nothing for hours, and Lev Kamenev, a Jewish intellectual who spoke unfathomable theories in a voice sounding like marbles dribbling into a tin washbowl. Others hoping for a share of power stood in descending orders of equality to the foot of the bier.

Leon Trotsky was nowhere to be seen, a bad blunder for someone anointed by Lenin to be his own successor to supreme power. Where in hell was Trotsky?

Comrade Alliluyeva was first among equals among the wives clustered at the front of the crowd surrounding the bier. Her gaze caught my eyes, and there was a slight flicker of recognition, but this was no time for smiles and waving.

Lenin's widow was the first to speak. Krupskaya rose from her seat, ascended the podium, and delivered a simple honest wish that those who followed Lenin to power would fulfill her husband's dreams for Socialism. She asked in Lenin's name that there be no statues and no commemorative paintings and no mausoleum in Red Square. I liked her.

Then Joseph Stalin mounted the podium as if the mantle of power were already his. The murmur of the crowd subsided.

"Comrades," Stalin began, "we Communists are people of a special cut. We have been made of peculiar stuff. There is no loftier title than that of a member of the party, of which Lenin has been founder and leader. It is not given to everyone to endure the hardships and storms that go with membership in such a party. Sons of the working class, sons of misery and struggle, and sons of heroic endeavor, above all, should be members of such a party."

Stalin's voice sometimes quavered, and he paused as if choked with emotion.

I could not help being moved by his words, though he spoke woodenly, like a Georgian peasant reciting the catechism in Russian. I smiled inwardly at his accent, yet I realized that Joseph Stalin was sincere in his commitment to fulfill all of Lenin's dreams—listed orally as if they were the Ten Commandments.

Then I glanced over to where Stalin's wife had stood and found her gone. For her to leave during her husband's eulogy to Lenin seemed a strange, even heretical, thing to do. Not being a fool, however, I stood rooted in place like everyone else until Stalin's speech ran its course.

I found myself not listening but looking at the great yearning, smelling, dirty masses who had gathered to pay tribute to their hope of deliverance, now dead. And they hoped desperately that this man, Joseph Stalin, would measure up to the greatness of Lenin

Stalin concluded, "We vow to thee, Comrade Lenin, that we shall not spare our lives in the endeavor to strengthen and broaden the alliance of the workers of the world—the Communist International. But first, we must begin at the beginning and build Socialism in one country, and that country is the Soviet Union."

Applause erupted and rose in ascending waves until it reached the level of a roar, then subsided to await the next speaker.

I realized that he had listed all of Lenin's goals and ended with his own as if it were Lenin's. It was clear that I had heard the essence of Stalin's commitment, and I was impressed.

"Comrade Makharov?" a soft voice inquired.

I turned to see Stalin's wife looking closely into my face to see if it was I. She was obviously nearsighted, and I loved it. The fur collar of her greatcoat was turned up to frame her face, and I swore before the Almighty—never having seen her face this close before—that I had never seen a more breathtaking beauty in my life. She emanated the scent of rose petals and whatever else women give off to arouse a man.

I smiled politely. "Comrade Alliluyeva."

She said, "I would like to talk to you about an important matter."

"And what might that be?"

She said, "It's confidential." She glanced about at the people standing nearby, then pointed to two columns of the Trade Union building that seemed to offer a private alcove for conversation. She lifted a finger for me to follow as she walked with quick feminine steps. I followed, watching her infinite grace.

When she turned to speak, I stopped her with a gesture to stare long and hard at a man who had drifted after us and stood within earshot. He got the message, shrugged, and walked away.

"Good for you," she said. "You are discreet and observant." Then she turned to face me, confident I would look out for her. Comrade Alliluyeva announced, "Today is only the beginning for the career of Joseph Stalin. He will ascend to supreme power and do for the Russian people what Abraham Lincoln did for the American people—liberate them from oppression. Stalin will lead the new Soviet Union to undreamed-of greatness and place it first among the nations of the world!" She paused for effect.

My jaw dropped slightly. I was startled by her vision and her passionate belief in her husband's destiny. This woman was a true believer in Joseph Stalin. When I regained composure, I asked, diffidently, "How does this relate to me?"

She said, "I have read your article on Lenin and four others published in scholarly journals. I found a copy of your book, *The Bloody Sunday of 1905,* and I am impressed by the quality of your writing. I am surprised that a writer of your liberal views was not sent to Siberia."

"Hiding well is a talent, too."

"You are excellent in research."

"So are you," I murmured, still in limbo. Comrade Alliluyeva was one of those charming people who filled in all the details before telling you what she was talking about.

"You show subtlety of mind in everything. Moreover," she emphasized, "I saw your sensitivity to others in the way you interviewed Lenin, dealt with Comrade Stalin, and treated your driver."

I yearned for a topic sentence to inform me what this was all about, but I smiled patiently and waited. There were worse things than standing there with a polite smile and listening to a lovely woman tell me how wonderful I was.

Comrade Alliluyeva drew herself up and got to the point. "I want to retain your services as a writer to do a biography of Joseph Stalin."

My face was in astonishment.

"Yes," she affirmed. "I have discussed the matter with my husband. He could not care less about having a biography written at this time, but he usually agrees with anything I want that will further his political career. I want you to be present as the chronicler of his growing greatness. Will you accept this assignment?"

Her proposal was so unexpected that, for a moment, I was speechless. I, Philip Makharov, to be the biographer of the man everyone seemed to fear?

She said, "You have not asked about compensation."

"What about compensation?"

She said, "Instead of being paid by the article for *Pravda,* you will be appointed to the staff and paid a handsome salary."

Sunshine spread over my heart.

"You will be assigned a car and a paid driver to take you safely to wherever you need to go to do your biographical research."

I grinned. "Victor will love it."

"You will have access to stores selling food and foreign goods unavailable to the average person. We want you to live well so you can write well."

That news should have made me happy, but I began to feel queasy about being more equal than others. Were privileges for the chosen few to be part of the new Socialist order?

Her luminous dark eyes smiled into mine. "Most of your research will be done with and through me," she said, "and you will call me Nadya, and I will call you Philip."

"It's a bargain," I said, scarcely believing my good fortune. This was the best funeral I had ever attended.

"Comrades," a voice said quietly.

We turned to see Joseph Stalin and realized that the building was almost empty.

I was startled to see that Stalin's eyes were red and swollen. He turned and looked at the bier of Lenin standing forlornly in the cavernous Hall of Trade Unions, seeming abandoned. When he looked back at us, his eyes were rimmed with tears, and I thought better of him.

Nadya impulsively reached out and lay her palm against his cheek. "We don't have to leave right away. Stay with him for a while."

Stalin nodded, embarrassed to have me see him like this, and turned to walk slowly back to the casket. Lenin's widow, Krupskaya, stood silently beside the bier, looking at the corpse of her late husband, now a yellow face on a white pillow. Stalin went around to the other side and stood quietly, his hand cradled in his greatcoat, staring at the face of Lenin. Krupskaya did not lift her gaze or say a word to acknowledge his presence. Stalin said not a word to her. They stood beside the casket in complete silence.

Nadya said quietly, "Your work on the biography of Joseph Stalin begins now."

I became alert.

"Do you see how Joseph Vissarionovich stands there, full of reverence and grief?"

"Did you hear his voice choke and quaver when he spoke the eulogy for Lenin?"

I nodded again.

"Stalin is mourning the death of his father."

"Not his *real* father" I blurted.

"His true father," she said. "A man of greatness may have several fathers in a lifetime: those he saw as role models for himself; those who shaped his outlook, his dreams, and his goals and advised him when he did not know where to turn; those who, when he stumbled, helped him to his feet and set him on the path that was right for him; those who were decisive in the crises of his life. These are all fathers to greatness. The death of a father is a shattering blow because it is like the death of part of oneself. Lenin was the father of Stalin in all those dimensions. Koba listened carefully to everything Lenin advised and did everything possible to live up to his standards. Lenin, in turn, appreciated Stalin's talents in administration and saw to it that he received recognition comparable to Trotsky. Koba was deeply grateful for that because he does not have it in him to match Trotsky's showmanship. Stalin is a diligent plodder in the very best sense who tries to do the right thing. Lenin sensed Koba's inferiority complex, especially next to flamboyant Trotsky, and constantly praised and encouraged him and gave him equal recognition. Lenin fed Stalin's soul."

I felt Lenin's will and testament about my calf and did not have the heart to say anything.

Nadya gestured toward Krupskaya and whispered, "Krupskaya hates Stalin. She took an instant dislike to him when they met and has been against him ever since. Koba brought gifts of melons and nuts to her and tried to be helpful, but she is a person for whom a dislike of someone is set in cement. Trotsky, on the other hand, could do no wrong. He was Lenin's boyhood friend and the brother she never had, and she fluttered around him with the best of everything. It was Krupskaya who worked on Lenin when he was sick and weak. It was she who urged him to renounce Stalin and give supreme power to Trotsky. She is a real curse to Stalin."

We looked for a long moment at the two enemies who loved Lenin and were loved by Lenin. And I realized that Stalin's wife was a person of sensitivity, compassion, and understanding, a human being in the fullest sense.

Nadya said, "When Lenin died, Stalin wept like a child who has lost his father. I stood there and watched him, and it broke my heart. There is one thing you can believe—Koba will fulfill the dreams of his dead father in creating a new Socialist order and a mighty Soviet Union."

My writing assignment had suddenly become interesting. I was won over: smitten by Stalin's wife and leavened by a new view of Joseph Stalin. Then I became aware again of Lenin's will and testament strapped to my calf—naming Trotsky to supreme power—and wondered if I should just dispose of it. Who would know but Victor, and he would say nothing, if only to preserve his pipeline to good things. I looked again at Lenin in his casket and knew I had to keep my word even if the action was risky. I would go to Leon Trotsky and let him read Lenin's will and testament and let him decide whether to challenge Stalin before the Party Congress.

After all, we historians are not supposed to make history. We only write about it.

5

Trust is the shield of children,
the oblivion of drunkards,
the hope of fools.
I am none of these.

—Joseph Stalin

Cold invaded through every pore of my skin, and I curled up even closer into a fetal position to try to warm myself. The shake and clatter of the railway car seemed to rub the frigidity of everything into the marrow of my soul, if I had one, to deny me peace. A boot nudged my shoulder, and I opened my eyes to glance up.

Hog said, "Comrade Stalin sent something for you to eat."

I sat up on the straw and was handed a brown paper package, which I unwrapped to find two cooked potatoes and a large sausage. I laughed out loud at Stalin's present. His first gift to me was a sausage, and the last gift was a sausage. Stalin was not without sardonic humor.

The two guards somehow reminded me of Victor, but my pocketknife was long gone, and so was Victor.

I asked Hog, "May I borrow your knife?"

He scoffed, "*Yob Tvoyu mat!*"

I said, "I suppose I could hold the sausage in the center and let you two chew off a third from either side," then I smiled.

A deep chuckle emanated from the Hog, and a panting wheeze came from Squeaky.

"Point your rifles at me, then hand me your knife," I said. "You won't regret it."

The two guards glanced at each other, then pointed their rifles at me. Hog pulled out a bayonet from its sheath and offered it to me handle first. They stood beyond any lunge I could make.

I carefully cut the sausage into three roughly equal sections, then offered a part to each of them, food being the ultimate gesture of goodwill in these terrible times.

"Stalin said the food was only for you!" Hog protested.

"Stalin will not know into whose stomach a sausage finds its way. Comrades should share."

The two guards glanced at each other, nodded, and each took a section of sausage. They stood in their greatcoats thoughtfully gnawing their meat, enjoying it enormously.

I chewed through my section and then munched through a cold potato. This was not like the sumptuous meals I had enjoyed as Stalin's biographer: smoked sturgeon, caviar with hard-boiled eggs on crackers, savory brown bread with pickled herrings, on and on and on, food for the privileged of the Soviet Union. And the presence of luminous Nadya, warm and womanly and giving. The food had gone, and so had Nadya. When I finished with eating the potato, I lay down into a fetal position on the straw to attempt some form of rest.

A moment later, a wool blanket floated down over me. I thanked Hog with a smile, and Squeaky too, after a second blanket fluttered down. They tucked the blankets in around the edges of me with their boots. Suffused in growing warmth, I drifted away into sleep. In the distance, I heard Hog say, "Sleep well, comrade." Then I slipped into memory.

Leon Trotsky was Stalin's enemy and a startling surprise when I met him. As the commander of the Red Army during the Civil War, he had outmaneuvered, outgeneraled, and outfought the White Army in every battle on every front. He saved the Bolshevik Revolution. His brilliant mind and his books had made him famous, and his fiery rhetoric could bring thousands of people to their feet with a roar. He was the stormy petrel of the revolution. I had expected to find Trotsky a towering, commanding figure on the order of Alexander Nevsky or Peter the Great.

What I found was a slight figure of middle height twisting nervously in his chair. He peered owlishly at me through pince-nez glasses. Trotsky unsettled me with his tired look, the unevenness of his voice, and his sick man's smile. His pale blue eyes seemed dark and violent behind his spectacles, his mouth twitched in a sardonic expression, and above his forehead towered a leonine shock of wavy black hair that bordered on the ridiculous.

Trotsky glanced up from his chair and sensed the unspoken question. He said, "I am sick with a very high temperature, and the doctors are at a loss to explain it. My illness incapacitates me at the most unexpected and critical moments."

I asked, "Is that why you did not attend Lenin's funeral?"

"I was in Odessa, very sick. Stalin called me and gave me the date and time of the funeral. I rose from my bed and traveled to Moscow, only to find that the date he had given me was the day *after* the funeral. He wanted me to miss the funeral and outrage everyone. The lying son of a bitch succeeded."

Trotsky took a handkerchief from his pocket to mop perspiration from his face in what was actually a cold room. Lenin's will and testament was in his lap. He had read Lenin's declaration appointing him to the pinnacle of power, and he was afraid—deathly afraid. He seemed frail.

Trotsky asked, "Does Comrade Stalin know of this?"

"Yes."

"Did you show this will and testament to him?"

"No, I hid it."

Trotsky barked, "Then how did he learn of it?"

"I was interviewing Lenin about an article for *Pravda* in which he announced his final decisions for succession of power. Stalin is the editor of *Pravda*. He was there when I came to show the first draft to Lenin, and he read it immediately."

"Let me see the article," Trotsky ordered, like his old self.

"Stalin took it from me almost forcibly and ordered me not to tell anyone of its contents."

Trotsky said, irritably, "Didn't you make a copy first?"

"There wasn't time. I wrote it under great pressure and had to bring it to Lenin almost before the ink was dry."

"And—"

"I was told by Stalin's wife that Lenin had had another stroke and could not see me. She ordered me to turn it over to Stalin for final disposition."

Trotsky said, "What was Stalin's wife doing there?"

"She was his aide and caretaker."

"Stalin doesn't miss a trick, does he?" Trotsky said. "Is she as pretty as I have heard?"

"More so," I said.

"Do you think she could have killed Lenin to further her husband's ambitions?"

"I don't think so… She's so lovely."

"Some women use their beauty to get what they want and to hide the devil within them."

"From what I have seen of her," I said, "she is loyal to her husband but fair to others. She is a genuinely good human being."

A long, thoughtful moment hung there, and then Trotsky said, "Your article announcing Lenin's decisions will never be published in *Pravda* or anywhere else."

I urged, "Lenin specifically asked that you read his will and trust at the next Party Congress. Then the whole world will know." Why, I asked myself, was I being forthright with this man when I lied or dissembled to everyone else? Honesty radiated from Trotsky, and it seemed to inspire honesty in me.

Anxiety shrouded his face. "Stalin will kill me or have me killed."

"Why do you say that? Stalin has never been known to kill anyone."

"Have you ever heard of the American writer, John Reed?" Trotsky said. "I know something about his death, and I know that he did not die of cholera as was announced."

I was surprised. "You mean, the author of *Ten Days That Shook the World* was murdered?"

Trotsky nodded. "Reed sent back an article to an American publication called *New Masses* in which he warned against the rise of

Joseph Stalin. Reed was killed to shut him up and cremated immediately so as not to have his body examined. Because of Reed's famous book, he was buried inside Kremlin walls as a 'hero' of the Soviet Union."

I said, "Writing the wrong thing in the Soviet Union can get the writer killed."

"Indeed it can," Trotsky said. "Now I want you to tell me every detail of what Stalin said and did when he discovered Lenin's decision to have me succeed him in supreme power."

I answered, "I have essentially told you everything. When he read the article and came to the part in which you had been appointed to the highest post, his face flushed red, and he read it again. His hand shook."

"Anger," Trotsky said. "Tell me more—his words, his reactions, everything."

"Stalin began to talk about his vision for the new Soviet Union. He said that he would create Socialism in one country to serve as a model for the workers of the world."

"That's preposterous!" Trotsky became agitated and rocked sideways in his chair. "There must be continuing agitation for revolution in all the developed nations in the world, or all the capitalists will surround us with a ring of steel. They will cut us off from all technical developments and strangle us economically!" He shouted, "WE MUST PULL DOWN ALL THE CAPITALIST COUNTRIES IN A WORLD-WIDE FIRE OF REVOLUTIONS!"

I stiffened as I remembered that my career and vital interests were on the side of Stalin. "Comrade Lenin said that the capitalists would sell us the rope to hang them with."

"That depends on who we are dealing with. Stalin is wrong in thinking he can create Socialism in one country without provoking the deadly enmity of the United States. Only perpetual revolution across the world can safeguard Socialism in the Soviet Union." He rocked in his chair as if a million Yankee soldiers were marching down the street.

Trotsky's passion startled me.

His pale blue eyes twinkled when he realized his effect on me. "Stalin is a pessimist," he said, "and that is why he pursues Socialism in one country. He does not believe in the popularity of Socialism with the masses because of his essentially dark view of mankind and society. The pessimist in power distrusts those whom he rules. He does not really believe that workers and peasants are truly capable of accepting Socialism unless it is rammed down their throats. Stalin is inclined to order the cure for the evils of capitalism without much regard for the patients' wishes. He once said that he thought eighty percent of the population would be the enemies of Socialism."

Trotsky laughed briefly. "As in everything, I am in the opposite camp from Stalin, with an outlook of cautious yet very real optimism. If the Communist Party pursues the right Socialist policies, the people will see the truth and support them. Sooner or later, the patients themselves, if well-informed, will see the evils of capitalism and will ask for the remedy of Socialism. Stalin is a revolutionary committed to the idea that he knows what is good for the people better than the people know what is good for themselves. And if they oppose his measures, he will grind them into the dirt."

I replied, "From what I have seen of that man, I am not sure I agree with you."

Trotsky replied grimly, "If Joseph Stalin gets control of the party, time will bear me out."

"And," I said, "that is why you will read Lenin's wishes at the Party Congress."

"PRECISELY!" he shouted, looking more like the winning general of the Red Army.

A woman materialized holding a tray of two cups and hot tea. "Teatime," she said.

Trotsky said to me, "This is Natalya Ivanovna, my darling wife." The warmth of his feelings for her radiated from his eyes and every fiber of his being.

Natalya Ivanovna ignored me to stare at her husband. "You are allowing yourself to become excited. You are perspiring. You will become sick again." She was a masterpiece of plainness: hair pulled back straight, face pale, dress of gray gingham over a dumpy figure, and Trotsky clearly adored her.

Trotsky nodded his thanks as he took the tray and put it on the desk and poured tea into two cups. Perspiration gleamed on his face, and the cup rattled on the saucer as he passed me a cup of tea.

She insisted, "You are getting sick with emotions."

Trotsky smiled and patted her cheek. "Comrade Makharov has fulfilled his revolutionary duty and will soon be on his way."

Natalya Ivanovna looked solemnly at me. "Leon is sick. You can see he is sick."

I nodded and smiled. "I'll be on my way after tea."

She looked gravely at Trotsky. "Cigars are not good for you either. Don't smoke them."

Trotsky laughed nervously. "One must live a little."

"My point exactly," she said sarcastically and plodded out.

There was not a cigar in sight, but the office was pungent with the stench of smoke permeating everything in the office.

Trotsky sipped his tea, and I sipped mine. Then he leveled his pale-eyed gaze at me and asked, "Did Stalin ask anything personal of you?"

"He asked if I would join him in building Socialism in one country, and I said yes."

Trotsky murmured, "Because you meant it or because you were afraid not to?"

"Both."

Trotsky shot me an edged look. "Did you come here as an agent for Stalin?"

"Of course not!" I blurted indignantly, putting my cup and saucer on the desk. "You saw me unstrap the will and testament from my leg. I lied to Stalin to keep my word to Lenin. Believe me, if Stalin had the slightest inkling that I had hidden Lenin's documents, I would not be here bringing them to you." I began to be really angry, and Trotsky could see it.

He asked, "What relationship do you have with Stalin other than writing for *Pravda?*"

"Comrade Alliluyeva commissioned me to begin a biography of Joseph Stalin."

Trotsky rocked his chair forward, and his feet came down on the floor with a slam. "You are Stalin's biographer, and you brought me these?" He held up Lenin's documents.

"I gave Lenin my word."

A wry smile played over Trotsky's mouth. "A brave and honorable man."

I shrugged, surprised to hear those words applied to someone I know as a liar and a coward.

Trotsky pulled a flat box out from his desk, opened the lid, and offered me a cigar. He said, "These were sent to me from Mexico by a marvelous artist named Diego Rivera, who is one of us. Take one."

I hesitantly took the panatela from the box and smelled the fragrance. Wonderful!

"Real Cuban cigars." Trotsky tossed me a box of matches and said, "Light up"—a gesture of goodwill that dissolved any tension between us.

I bit off the tip of the cigar, put it into my mouth, lighted it, drew deeply, and exhaled the most savory smoke imaginable. I said, "This is absolutely exquisite."

"A reward for a decent man."

"I only did what I had to do."

"You sell yourself short."

Trotsky rocked back in his chair again and looked at me with appraising eyes. He had a curious talent for making me feel like an object, or a fly on the wall, as he talked to me. I remembered the rumors that Trotsky was so much a man of theory and ideology that he could not relate personally to most people. He was blunt, abrasive, sarcastic, almost unaware of the feelings of others. We live in a world of feelings, and lacking a sense of empathy for other people could be a fatal flaw in Russian politics. Trotsky could command armies, but he could not connive, insinuate, or manipulate people. He could not build coalitions as a politician must because the talent for it was not in him. Cunning was not part of Leon Trotsky's psyche, but as I learned, there was little else in Stalin.

Then Trotsky said, gently, "Did Comrade Lenin have anything personal to say to me."

"He said something strange. He said, 'Ask Leon Trotsky to bring me a brace of ducks for dinner in the spring.'"

Trotsky grinned, and then his stomach began to pulsate. He threw back his head and burst into metallic laughter. His voice sounded like a horse galloping over an iron bridge. He guffawed until tears came to his eyes, and he looked wonderfully human. When he calmed down, he looked first to see if Natalya Ivanovna was hovering outside the office, then took a cigar for himself to light and enjoy.

Trotsky said, "In that request, tinged with sly good humor, is the living, breathing Lenin. In that jest is my beloved Vladimir, friend of my youth and the great comrade of my life. If you have a moment, let me tell you of our hunting days, before Vladimir Ilyich Ulyanov became Lenin and Lev Davidovich Bronstein became Trotsky. The story of two young men who became fast friends while hunting together and worked as one for Socialism. True friends."

This was something new. These men were so famous for so long that it seemed they were born as white marble statues. Could they ever have been young and foolish?

Trotsky reminisced through a flume of tobacco smoke. "We used to go to the river Dubna where, in the spring, the river flooded the countryside to form shallow lakes and marshes bordered by reeds. In the springtime, the waters were swarming with ducks and geese of all kinds, with many snipe and curlew. Nearby, in the small woods, one could hear woodcocks clucking in the bilberry shrubs. We took turns paddling with a single oar, the other holding the shotgun, looking for a fresh feather floating in the water that meant ducks were nearby. The boat was so light and shaky that it was chancy to stand up when firing the shotgun. We usually kneeled, fired, and paddled over to retrieve the bird."

Trotsky chuckled in his reverie. "Once, when Vladimir had the shotgun and I the paddle, a brace of mallards appeared flying low and fast over the reeds. He forgot himself and leaped to his feet and accidentally fired both barrels at once. The recoil knocked him flying backwards into the water. He came up spluttering, 'Get the ducks! Get the ducks!' His doubled shot had hit both of the mallards, and we retrieved them. Because Vladimir was soaked and muddy, our shooting was over for the day. We went to his home where his wife, Krupskaya, plucked the birds and cooked them in a marvelous Madeira sauce. We ate them for dinner with lemon vodka and roared with laughter at Vladimir's expense, who laughed at himself in marvelous good humor. We talked through half the night planning for the revolution and the utopia that would arise with Socialism."

I realized that Trotsky was living in another time and place and that I had ceased to be there. For a long moment, the past lived in smoke until Trotsky murmured, "I cannot believe he is dead. Will good times never come again?"

Then he rejoined me and arose to his feet. His pale eyes became impersonal, and I felt that I was again a speck on the wall. He said, primly, "What can I give you as a genuine reward for the risk you took in bringing the documents to me?"

"You can read Lenin's will and testament at the coming Congress of Soviets."

"Will you stand with me against Stalin?"

"No, comrade. I know where my bread is buttered."

Trotsky chuckled. "An honest answer from an honest man."

"Thank you," I said. "But now I must go, and you have not answered Lenin's request."

Trotsky drew himself up and said, "To honor the ghost of Vladimir Ilyich Ulyanov—and stop Stalin in his tracks—I will read Lenin's will before the Congress of Soviets and do all in my power to carry it out... And tell Krupskaya that I will bring a brace of ducks in the spring to share in the memory of someone we both loved."

I was deeply touched. This was the old Leon Trotsky, slayer of lions and leader of men.

Trotsky became alert. "How did you come here?'

"A driver dropped me off about two city blocks from here, and I walked over," I said. "The driver is waiting for me."

"That means the people who are shadowing me don't know who you are or where you came from, but they will follow you out to your driver. Can you trust your driver?"

"I share everything I get with him," I said.

"Good," Trotsky said, scooping up a half dozen cigars and stuffing them into my pockets. "Share these with him… Now follow me."

We arose and went out of his apartment and clattered down a flight of stairs to the door facing the street. But instead of going outside, Trotsky led me to a small door to what was apparently a closet under the stairwell. He pushed aside an assortment of junk and pulled out a panel in the rear to reveal a low corridor leading to the back of the building.

Trotsky said, "This corridor goes through this building and through the next and opens between two buildings onto the far street. I never use it because I may need it someday for an escape, and I do not want my enemies to know it exists. I have seen enough of you to know you will not reveal it to anyone."

We shook hands, and I stooped down to enter the corridor. As I scooched awkwardly through the causeway, all I could think about was the astonishing realization that this impersonal man, this great man, had made a snap decision to entrust me with a secret that could endanger his own life. If Stalin knew about the causeway, he could trap Trotsky like a rat and kill him.

The far end of the corridor opened through a small door to a narrow space between two buildings. I crawled out, closed the door, and went out to the street to look carefully up and down at every door, window, and alcove. The way was clear. I walked the longest possible route to come back to Victor and the car from the opposite direction.

Victor was dozing in the driver's seat when I opened the passenger door and crawled in. Victor awakened with a start as I pulled out six cigars and gave him three.

"Cuban cigars," I said. "Comrades should share."

6

> Should I be less than they
> who cast long shadows over Russia,
> less than Ivan the Terrible
> and Peter the Great?
> I will not squander this chance
> to eclipse all who have gone before.
>
> —Joseph Stalin

Nadya's image in the rain-fogged window vaporized when Victor beeped the horn outside. The time had come to drive over to hear Leon Trotsky read Lenin's will and testament designating him as successor to supreme power over the Soviet Union. My historian soul whispered that I would be present at an occasion of enormous importance, a watershed in the history of the world. As we drove through the city, I absorbed into memory the conditions of the city for the book I would one day write.

During the short days of January, under dull gray skies, the sleet began to fall incessantly and slushed everything. The mud was thick, clinging, and slippery, tracked everywhere by boots. Dank winds rushed in from the north, and a damp, penetrating fog rolled through the streets, making even those in fur coats shiver as if naked. Streetlights were few and far between. Electric lights in private homes had power only from six o'clock until ten in the evening, and power failed frequently. Most buildings were dark because candles were dear, and there was little kerosene to be had. Night came down swiftly as in every corner of the city; in every open space, groups of soldiers, peasants, workers, and students argued, argued, argued.

Victor knew the rules of the game and dropped me off at some distance from the meeting. Being chauffeured to the door was not the thing to do in days of desperation when the country was falling apart and ordinary people struggled to survive under appalling conditions.

When I turned the corner, I could see hundreds of people streaming into the gaunt brick walls of a huge unfinished building. I crowded through the doors with the others to find mobs of black-clothed workers packed around a scaffolding draped in red, their simple faces upturned toward the podium. Here were the masses who lived on a daily ration of a quarter pound of black bread, while speculators and merchants took advantage of the chaos to pile up fortunes and spend them on luxuries and *every* form of self-indulgence. Someone had scrawled on the brick wall, "Save Russia!—Kill the Capitalists!"

I glanced toward the rear of the building. The cavernous brick shell was crowded with rough, dirty workers, barrel-shaped women in *babushkas*, soldiers splattered with mud and some with bloodstained bandages. The air was so foul with the stench of unwashed people in unwashed clothing that I could scarcely breathe. A low-voiced hum of talk filled a building that was, ironically, warmed by the sheer mass of bodies present. Pale light oozed from kerosene lamps, and occasional light bulbs flickered over the mobs of people awaiting the arrival of Leon Trotsky. The mood of everyone was bleak and gloomy because the light of Lenin's leadership had gone out. The man who had promised that gold would be used to make public urinals in the new Socialist order was dead.

Two companies of Red Guards came swinging through the entrance, tramping stiffly in their greatcoats and singing a loud marching chorus such as the *Yunkers* used to sing under the Tsar. They marched in place for a moment, looking military, until the Red commander ordered them to halt and fall out.

I noticed that the Red Guards all carried rifles at the ready, and the officer wore a pistol. They quietly positioned themselves at strategic places around the podium, at front and rear entrances, and every ten feet or so along the walls. A single row of seats had been set up and roped off for important individuals, and a Red Guard stood behind each seat, at attention, holding his rifle.

What was going on?

"Comrade Makharov?" a soft voice inquired. I glanced into the nearsighted eyes of Nadya looking closely to see if it was I, a closeness that gave me the internal wallop I had learned to expect when meeting her. She smiled exquisitely from within the fur collar she had turned up as if hiding cozily therein.

She added, "So you came after all."

"This is a great historic moment, and as Stalin's biographer, I should be here." I felt no obligation to add that I wanted to see what happened when Trotsky made his presentation and what Stalin's response would be.

"I suppose so," she said uncertainly, then asked, "Have you seen Koba?"

"Didn't you come with him?" I asked.

"No," she said, pulling her collar closer to frame her lovely face. "He has been meeting with other leaders at party headquarters and is coming straightaway here."

A stern voice cut in indignantly: "What are you doing here?"

When I saw Stalin, I began to answer, but he was glaring at Nadya.

She shrank a little, then flattened down her collar and turned defiantly to face her husband. "I am a revolutionary woman—an ideological woman! This is a turning point in the history of all the Russias, and I have a right to be here and do my part!

Stalin snapped, "We have been through all this before. Tonight will be an ugly business, and I do not want you here. And," he stressed, "you are the mother of two small children who need your attention!"

I was surprised. She had not mentioned two small children to me.

Nadya said defiantly, "I have engaged a nana to look after them."

"A nana who can neither read nor write," Stalin snapped.

"So what? She can feed them, clean them, clothe them, take them to the park to play with other children."

"They are not infants," he insisted. "They are in school and need your attention. Svetlana brought me her homework papers to sign, and they were full of errors!"

Nadya flashed, "Then why didn't you sit down with Svetlana and help her correct the errors? You are her father, and it is as much your responsibility as mine."

Stalin's face reddened. "I was on my way to party headquarters to meet with Zinoviev and Kamenev and prepare for tonight's political action. The future leadership of the Soviet Union will be decided here, and I could not take the time to correct a child's homework."

Her temper rose. "I could not take the time either because I had to come here to play a woman's part in the revolution!"

Stalin's voice became even more edged. "I have the responsibility for controlling the party here, tonight, and you have no responsibilities here whatever! Svetlana is doing poorly in school, and Vassily is fighting with his teachers and other children all the time. They are running wild because they are not being nurtured and supervised. Your children need a mother's attention, and you should be home attending to them!"

I stepped quietly back, appalled to be present during this domestic squabble.

Nadya was defiant. "Women are the equals of men in the new Socialist order. If I, as a liberated woman, choose to be here tonight for Socialism, I have right to be here!" She paused for effect, then hissed, "I am a liberated woman."

Stalin fired back, "You are not liberated from your responsibilities as a mother, and you never will be."

Nadya lowered her voice. "You did not worry about my maternal obligations when you asked me to be Lenin's aide and nurse. Then you wanted to know everything that happened with Lenin for your own political game. What happened to the children then was their problem!"

I could see how that stung, and I groaned inwardly. I did *not* want to be present at this seriously ugly row.

Infuriated, Stalin barked, "As your husband, I order you to go home and attend to the needs of Svetlana and Vassily."

"I will not!" she almost shouted. "I belong here as a revolutionary woman of the Communist Party. I will not take orders from an arrogant husband!"

Stalin lived up to his name, man of steel. "As your superior in the party, I order you to go home and attend to your children."

"No!" she said, but wilted a little.

"An order by your superior in the party must be obeyed. You know that. If you continue to refuse, I will have you stripped of rank and expelled from the party. Then you will be nothing!"

Nadya's eyes filled with tears, and she began to weep. She turned away and ran to the entrance with her face in her hands to disappear into the milling crowd outside.

Stalin watched her leave with the eyes of an unhappy husband. He would have a cold bed tonight, and the fight would leave scars on their marriage.

I felt awful, but there was nothing I could do except wish I could disappear. I made a biographer's mental note that Joseph Stalin bullied his wife into submission and did not hesitate to humiliate her publicly.

Stalin turned to me and said, "This should be considered a private matter between husband and wife."

"My lips are sealed," I said.

"And your pen?"

"Dry," I lied.

Stalin's dark paranoiac eyes bored into mine. "Good things will come if I can trust you. Worse things than you can imagine if I cannot."

I smiled weakly and groveled. "I am your biographer," I said, as if this statement would assure that I would live long enough to write it. A strange thought straggled through my brain. Trotsky and I may be the only two people here who know that Stalin had John Reed killed, yet everyone seemed afraid of him as if they instinctively knew that Stalin could and would kill anyone who stood in his way. I could see it in the fearful deference of those who talked to him.

The hum of voices in the building rose to a thundering wave of cheers and cries of "Trotsky! Trotsky! A Novaya Rus! [For New Russia!]"

We turned to see Leon Trotsky striding toward the chair marked with his name.

Trotsky walked alone, without bodyguards or entourage. He walked with the quick strides of someone who knew he was right, with the irritating confidence and abrupt manner of those who felt that the opinions of others did not count. His was the arrogance that was devoid of vanity, but convinced that his knowledge was the only true knowledge, his view the only right view.

Stalin watched Trotsky with unforgiving eyes. Lenin, his spiritual and intellectual father, had passed over Stalin to give supreme power to this Jew.

Trotsky stopped for a moment at his chair to glance at the armed Red Guard standing beside it, then he pulled away the rope and sat down. He pulled out a sheaf of papers from an inside pocket and began to read what could only be Lenin's will and testament.

Even at this distance, looking at him from the shadow of the podium, I could see Trotsky's face glistening with perspiration and his shirt soaked in sweat. Was this the debilitating illness he had told me about, or was he afraid? Trotsky squirmed around in his seat and repeatedly crossed and uncrossed his legs. He glanced backward at the Red Guard soldier, rifle in hand, and twitched a look at the Red Guards officer who stared down at him.

The officer walked quietly over and sat beside Trotsky in the front row. The crowd could not see the officer slip the revolver out of its holster and then lay it in his lap under the edge of his greatcoat. The officer murmured something to Trotsky.

Trotsky stiffened in his chair, placing both feet squarely on the floor, staring straight ahead with eyes opened wide. I could see that he was frightened, and his huge shock of hair seemed to be standing on end. I was watching a threat to assassinate. Only Stalin and I could see it, and only I was concerned that a fine man had been given a choice of life or death.

As I watched Trotsky squirming, I sensed, again, a childlike frailty, a man possibly not up to the burden of greatness. I wondered if his reputation as a fearless man of action was a consequence of his famous self-discipline rather than an expression of his instinct. My impressions in his office returned: brilliant intellect; absence of vanity; fairness in judgments even of his enemy, Stalin; and something in him that resembled the tragic hero of Aristotle's *Poetics*—a superior person with a tragic flaw that brings him down to destruction. Trotsky had not made a single move since Lenin died that was not a political blunder. What would Trotsky do now when he was charged with reading Lenin's will before the Party Congress, naming him to lead the new Soviet Union?

Trotsky answered my question by standing up suddenly and striding toward the entrance. The officer stood up with him and walked closely after—his hand inside his greatcoat.

Disbelief rumbled through the crowd, who understood that Trotsky was leaving the fray, and aghast cries of *"Prosim! Prosim! Prosim!* [PLEASE! PLEASE! PLEASE!]" roared through the building as the two men strode toward the door. Workers and peasants and party members spilled out of the crowd to run forward and beg him not to leave. One old worker grabbed his sleeve, and Trotsky stopped, momentarily, until the officer poked something into his back, and he pulled away from the worker to walk toward the door. The aged worker stood, disbelieving, tears streaming from his eyes.

The crowd became angry and chanted, *"Posor* TROTSKY! POSOR TROTSKY! [SHAME ON TROTSKY! SHAME ON TROTSKY!]"

Leon Trotsky seemed suddenly to panic and hurled himself out the door to disappear into the night. The officer watched Trotsky until he was gone, then glanced at Stalin with a wry smile. Stalin nodded quietly with approval.

I was shocked to see Lenin's heir apparent run for his life. It was an historian's dream, in a sense, to see the course of history change before one's eyes. The threat to kill Trotsky was probably a bluff, but it worked and eliminated Stalin's great rival from the political arena. Had Trotsky been killed, the officer would have been torn to pieces by the workers, peasants, and soldier present who worshipped

Trotsky. I could scarcely believe that the hero general of the Red Army, victor in a hundred battles, had lost his nerve. Perhaps he was so sick that his mind was addled. Who knows? Who will ever know?

Religion does not play the role it should in my life, but I said an inner prayer to whomever might be out there to spare this brilliant but flawed man from a tragic end. And I added a peasant's farewell: *Slava Bogu,* Glory to God.

The crowd began to break up and rumble toward the entrance as if the evening had ended.

Stalin stepped forward with his arms raised and shouted to the crowd, "COMRADES! COMRADES! NOTHING HAS CHANGED! TONIGHT WE WILL BEGIN WORK TO CARRY FORWARD LENIN'S PLAN TO CREATE A SOCIALIST STATE IN ONE COUNTRY. THE NEW SOVIET UNION WILL BECOME A PARADISE FOR WORKERS, PEASANTS, AND SOLDIERS IF WE ACT AS ONE... LISTEN TO ME!"

The appeal worked. I could sense the despair lifting from the crowd at the grandeur of his words. Two men came forward to join him: Zinoviev, the orator and demagogue with popular appeal; and Kamenev, the academician with a solid brain trained in matters of Marxist doctrine. The three men faced the crowd, joined their hands, and raised them over their heads, shouting in unison, "A *Rus!* [FOR RUSSIA!]"

The crowds raised clenched fists in the Communist salute and roared, "A *Rus!*"

Someone began to sing "The Internationale," and everyone joined in:

> We will destroy the world of oppression to
> the ground, and only then will we build our own
> New World. Who was nothing will then become
> everything.

The building shook with the bellows of revolutionary voices, fierce and impassioned.

Migod! I thought, absolutely thrilled. *I am here at the very creation of a new world!* I forgot about the filth and degradation and rancid stench of unwashed masses. I was present at the birth of a great new nation in an epoch that would change the course of history!

I would write shelves of books about our time and become an historian ranking with Herodotus. What a glorious age to be alive!

Stalin mounted the podium and spoke first. "Building Socialism in one country is our first task. To do this, we must make of the Soviet Union an iron-hard monolithic fortress that can withstand the coming attacks from capitalistic nations. All of us must work together as one, every person in place and marching as one with everyone else. We must all be immune from petty self-serving individualism."

I smiled inwardly at his speaking style in which the words seemed chiseled in wood. As his speech droned on, I became aware of someone very different from the others.

A lovely young woman was quietly working her way from the front of the crowd to the line facing the podium. Her eyes were turquoise in color, almond shaped, and long blond hair cascaded from under her *schlepki,* a lambswool hat. She walked leaning slightly backward to carry the weight of full breasts on a petite body but had the small hands and delicate feet of a Willendorf Venus. She wore a fur coat and stylish boots, a dangerous way to dress in these times and this place, but she walked with the grace of one who knew that a pretty face and stunning torso made her immune to shabby treatment. In this grungy crowd, she seemed a flower growing out of a sewer.

When she reached the throngs facing the podium, she turned and smiled upward. For as long as Stalin spoke, she continued her pearly smile. When Zinoviev and Kamenev took their turns to speak, the smile vanished, and she fidgeted in boredom. Her interest was only in Joseph Stalin.

After the speeches and the singing were done, the three men descended from the podium. The lovely young woman skipped forward to plant a kiss on Stalin's mouth.

I did not know who she was, and I did not want to know. The women that Stalin poked himself into were his private affairs and of no interest to this historian. This woman merely proved again that fame was a powerful aphrodisiac and that Joseph Stalin was like most men in exploiting the attentions of desirable women who flutter around the flames of glory. But I wondered, *Was she the reason Nadya was sent home in tears?*

Yet I had to interview him about the events of this evening to include in my forthcoming biography of Joseph Stalin. I worked my way through the crowd surging around him and shouted to him, "When can I see you for an interview?"

He turned and looked me squarely in the eyes. Stalin's veneer of charm and folksiness became translucent, and I quailed before what I sensed beneath it. He softened a little, the corners of his moustache curling upward in a practiced smile. After all, it would not do to terrorize one's biographer. He said, firmly, "Nadya knows much about the early years. Talk to her for now, and we will get together later."

I smiled too much. "Yes, yes, a good suggestion."

"Philip," he intoned.

"Yes?"

"Don't ever interrupt me again."

"I won't, I won't. Never again!"

I backed away and let the crowd surge around him. Stalin had made an excellent suggestion: "Talk to Nadya." Wonderful! He had given me reason to talk to her, spend time with her, come to know her. And I longed to know her. The Great Man could not complain that I was interested in his lovely wife when it was he who had directed me to see her. The situation was pregnant with possibilities, and I turned to my task hopefully aroused.

7

> The god of the North awakened and rubbed
> the dust of a thousand years from his eyes.
> "Where?" he roared, "is my Slavic warrior?"
> "Slain," I replied, "by a woman's embrace."
>
> —Joseph Stalin

I remember as if it were yesterday when I arrived at the apartment of Nadya and Stalin for the first of my meetings to do research on the early years of Joseph Stalin for his biography.

I waved my credentials nervously at two guards who looked strong enough to pick up a bull by the horns. Nadya appeared at the front door at almost the same time, carrying a bulging bag of something that smelled good. She smiled her hello and unlocked the drab door into an apartment that was a revelation: handsomely carved antique furniture, luxurious drapes over the windows, plush astrakhan rugs on a hardwood floor, an ornate samovar on a low table whose surface was exquisitely inlaid with ivory designs, and really fine paintings on the wall. This was not the austerity I had expected from the bleakness of his office and the gravitas of his personality. I was drawn to a large painting of Jesus greeting the Russian people.

"Koba loves art," she said, "but the rest of it is my doing. He could not care less about comfort and luxury. He would sleep on the floor as long as he has a place to work."

I admired the painting and wondered, *Does Stalin love Jesus too?* I was scarcely prepared for sacred art here. I supposed the hope of salvation lurked in us all, and the temptation to pray must be nearest in those who live with the threat of death.

TO SOME ABSENT GOD

Nadya put water into the samovar and prepared it for making tea, then put out the cups and saucers with fine silverware. She was dressed in good Communist gray, in a suit exquisitely tailored to flatter her slender figure. I was sure she had the finest tailor in the city eager to garb the lovely woman and please the great man. Finally, Nadya unpacked the food from the bag and spread it before me on ornate plates. Her movements were swift and impulsive over the food, and she moved with the grace of a Bolshoi ballerina. Nadya was one of those people whose face was disturbingly different from side and front views. In profile, she was an austere regal beauty; *en face*, she was girlish and charming. I was awed by her attractiveness every time we met. Then I saw the food.

Migod! I thought. Caviar. Canned sturgeon. Ham. Smoked salmon. Wonderful *kasha*, black bread whose aroma smelled like the elixir of life. Fresh fruit was unobtainable anywhere in Moscow this miserable winter, and yet here on the table were oranges and bananas…bananas!

This was *kremlinlevsky payok*—the Kremlin ration—writ in colossal letters. Here was *blat,* access to secret stores that ordinary people could only dream about as they cursed the bread and did without the meat. My eyes were bigger than my head, but not as large as my appetite.

She smiled and rewarded my astonishment with a serene touch of her lips upon my forehead, Russian style, thrilling me. "I bought this for you at Koba's direction. He was concerned about having to push you away because of urgent business. He admitted that he had been rude and wanted you to know that as his biographer and friend, you were welcome in his home. Koba wants you to enjoy these delicacies and only then talk about the early years."

"My thanks to the man of steel," I mumbled. For the next hour, I made a pig of myself and devoured plate after plate of flavors I had forgotten, washed down with vodka—the very best vodka, I might add. If Stalin wanted to buy my soul with such food, he had made a bargain with me, a Faustian bargain, but worth it from a taste bud's point of view. When I had finished with fish, bread, and fruit, she served little honey cakes with strong piping hot tea.

My innards satisfied by anything in memory, I turned to her expectantly. It was time to begin. I was not one of those writers who take copious notes because stopping to write would interrupt the flow of human interaction. I remember afterward what was important and did not wish to bog down in details being scribbled at the time.

I knew that Nadya could recount those things she had personally experienced, and that at least was a start in breathing life into the biography of the man who had begun to look over the Soviet Union. I had noticed at first meeting that Stalin was almost three decades older than Nadya, which was not surprising among successful men in middle age who often took young women as wives to display as trophies of their greatness. She either did not notice or did not care that his face was pockmarked and his skin the color of dirt. He was anything but a handsome heartthrob to women, but did not need to be. Glory is handsome enough and fame a powerful aphrodisiac. I was surprised to discover that she had known him from earliest childhood.

"How long have I known him?"

Nadya responded, "For as long as I can remember." Her eyes went dreamy soft, and her lips puckered slightly as if expecting a kiss, which took an act of will not to give. "My parents—my mother, actually—offered their home as a sanctuary for the revolutionaries when the secret police were close after them. The rebels used it as the safe house of last resort in order to protect my parents from the Tsar's *Okhrana*. My earliest memories are of bearded wild-eyed men pounding at our door. My mother, who was a radical Communist, gave them meals and a place to sleep. Usually, they stayed only overnight, but sometimes, Koba was around for days or even weeks."

"What did Stalin do when he stayed with your family?"

"Most often, he burst in with his comrades, gulped down a meal, slept on the floor, and went forth the next day to the attack. I was very young, and he seemed to me a giant. Once I watched my mother strap his two revolvers across the back so they could not be seen from the front under his greatcoat. She had stitched little straps on the holster that prevented the guns from falling out in that position. When the time came to draw his pistols, he would reach around to the back and come out fighting. Before he left on his mission, though, he always picked me up and kissed me on the mouth and then kissed my mother's hand."

I smiled wryly. "I don't think of Joseph Stalin as being either fatherly or chivalric."

Nadya opened her large eyes even wider. "That shows how little you know about Koba. I remember times, when I was only a toddler, when he would bathe me and tuck me into my bed and kiss me good night. He had warm, soft eyes and the gentlest of hands. A thoughtful giving man. I remember the presents he brought to us unexpectedly: a loaf of bread, part of a ham, a chicken, half a salmon, sometimes caviar, things that were unobtainable, but he got them somehow and gave them to us. When he was gone a long time, we would live on a heel of bread and a hunk of cheese or a cucumber with a little brine left on it. It seemed that whenever we had reached the absolute bottom of desperation, facing starvation, Koba would stride through the door with a bag of potatoes, or better. And always there was something special for me. He never forgot me: rolls, candy, something delicious. Whenever possible, he brought me sugared nuts—I was mad about them."

"I would say that you began to fall in love with him at the earliest possible age."

"Earlier." She smiled, giggling adorably, like a teenager. "He would spread out what he had brought us on the table for everyone to see. Then he would pick me up and place me astride his shoulders and prance about as if he were my pony. How I squealed with delight. Sometimes, he would sit down on the floor with his back against a bench and play bail with me. Best of all were the pillow fights in which he would throw a pillow at me and knock me over. Then I would throw a pillow at him, and he would fall over as if hit by a locomotive. Sometimes, Mother would sit on the floor too and join in for a pillow free-for-all. How we laughed, what fun we had, how we loved our wonderful Koba. He was the sun that warmed and illuminated those grim times."

I thought that this was scarcely credible *pi'zhdun*, knowing what I did about Stalin, but I said, "You haven't mentioned your father. Was he also a radical?"

"No. Sergei Yakovlevich was not at all happy about being involved in the revolution. He was an engineer, but not a man of vision and passion. Food, drink, work, sex, and a place to sleep were all he asked of life. As long as he had these basics, he did not give a damn about high ideals. Koba always brought a bottle of vodka to drown the fear he saw in my father's eyes. The threat of prison or death if we were caught hung over my father constantly like an ominous cloud. Whenever Koba or other revolutionaries came to stay, he was so afraid of what might happen that he drank himself to sleep almost every night. He was pallid and oozed perspiration until his smell filled the room. Lenin stayed with us once, and he was more afraid than ever. He was my father, but I was not proud of him. He was a cringer who hid himself in the dark."

This was pretty brutal condemnation from a daughter, but when compared to the fearlessness of Joseph Stalin… "Why did he put up with his wife being involved in the revolution?"

"My mother, Olga, married him on the condition that he join the Communist Party and participate in the struggle. She kept the house and cooked the meals and gave him sex when he wanted it, but she did not love him. Father was her means of support, and that freed her to devote herself to the revolution. The times he went away for months to work on an engineering project were the happiest times for her."

"Trading her physical self to him for the cause."

"Of course. Sex is nothing. The triumph of the proletariat is everything."

Nadya's dismissal of sex triggered a flicker of carnal hope that she might casually dispense some to me. But I kept my mind focused on research. She was giving me a peek into the revolutionary years of Joseph Stalin that I could never have imagined him being a part of. It seemed so out of character with the man of steel that had I heard it from someone else, I would have called it a lie, a sham created to be included in a spurious legend of the Great Man. Inwardly, I resisted what she said. Either it was true, though, or Nadya was the greatest actress in the Soviet Union. She had told me what seemed to be actual events surrounding her earliest years of knowing Stalin. I would not be human if I did not understand—since these were factual events—why she had come to love him. Stalin had courted her virtually from the cradle and shaped her into what he wanted in a woman—a kind of Pygmalion.

The notion that that ominous bastard doted on a mother and her child in the midst of a revolution would read well, and I duly filed it in the archives of my brain. I suppose that even the most brutal of men have something within them that responds with kindness when faced with a Madonna and child.

"One day, my father went out and never returned," she said. "We have not the slightest idea what happened to him. Perhaps he died in the chaos of that time and the fighting in the streets, or he was killed somewhere on an engineering project. Perhaps the fear was too much, and he ran away. Who knows? As a consequence, Mother and I were completely dependent on Koba. He never let us down. There was always food on the table and money for rent. Then my mother developed schizophrenia, which runs in the family, and one day, she took her own life. Koba stepped in and became more of a father to me than my own father had been."

"When did he become a man to you?"

"It was a gradual thing. As I entered my teens, feelings grew that I did not understand, but I knew that I longed to see him and be with him. Feelings that were different from those one would have for an adopted father. He came to mean so much more to me than just an older man who had taken care of me. I began to feel passion for him. My parents had virtually had sex in front of me, and I knew what it was all about, so to speak. I knew that I wanted him as a lover and husband and protector. One afternoon, and this is not for publication, I seduced him in a way he could not refuse."

"How was that?"

"I appeared before him without clothing and began to kiss and caress him."

"How old were you?"

"Fourteen."

I was shocked. Nadya had been almost a child.

"We were married when I was seventeen. He wanted to do the right thing."

"Have you ever known another man?"

"No. I am Stalin's wife, and as long as I am, there will never be anyone else."

I envied her husband.

Her eyes widened and rimmed with tears. "There is someone else for him."

"What?"

She looked down for a moment and then said, "There is another woman in my husband's life." She looked as if she could die.

"I don't believe it. He has you, and trust me, no man would ask for more."

"It's true," she insisted. "The poem I showed you that began, 'Tell me now to go away and never come again' was not written for me. I came across a box of love poems, and none of them had been given to me. They were written for someone else. I copied one or two, and that was what I showed you. There *is* someone else." She whimpered. "Please, please, find out who she is."

What an assignment. I was retained by Stalin's wife to write a biography of Joseph Stalin, only to receive an additional commission to snoop into his other life, whatever that was, to find the "other woman." I remembered the lovely blonde who had skipped up to Stalin and kissed him at the Party Congress, and I wondered. Surely this was the most banal of jobs. What man ever attained Stalin's level of power without having lovely women climb into his bed? What fool would be dumb enough to poke around in the dark corners of the life of a man as dangerous as Soso Djugashvili? What man having a wife as beautiful as Nadya would have the energy to pursue another woman? I would have exhausted myself in her.

But Nadya begged me, and spineless literati that I was, I agreed. I had not the faintest notion how to carry out her request. I decided to legitimately pursue the materials needed for Stalin's biography and allow destiny to decide whether I should find another woman lurking under his bed. It would be damned unhealthy for me if I did.

8

You there, who smile at me.
Do you really think
that I believe what I see
and offer my broad back
as your target?
Think again.

—Joseph Stalin

"The whore," I murmured as a hump in the railroad tracks and the clickety-clack awakened me to frigid darkness. I lifted my head to look around for the guards. Snoring drew my gaze to a shape huddled in one corner where Hog slept, embracing his rifle. Heavy breathing drew my glance to another corner where Squeaky slept, using his rifle, piled-up straw, and his *schlepki* as a pillow. Both guards rocked in their sleep to the rhythms of the moving train.

Icy wind numbed my face, and I traced it to one door of the railroad car that had jiggled open to the width of a foot or so—open enough for a leap outside to freedom. Quietly I threw back my blankets, slipped on my boots, rewrapped myself in blankets, and padded over to the open door.

I peered outside into a dark landscape of trees and rocks and gullies flashing by in the blurs of night. A dangerous jump, with one chance in a hundred that I would land without breaking a leg or worse. And if I did land without injury, the only directions I could take would be to follow the tracks to wherever Stalin's men would be waiting for me. Only a fool would strike out blindly across the taiga wilderness in winter to die, in freezing misery in the middle of nowhere.

"No-you-don't!" Hog's voice barked as the cold end of a rifle barrel poked into my neck.

"Don't what?" I blurted, groping for an alibi.

"Don't jump!"

"Jump?" I scoffed. "Do you think I am crazy enough to leap out there and break every bone in my body?"

"Why are you standing at the open door?"

"Would you rather I pissed in the car?"

"What about your bucket?"

"I couldn't find it in the dark," I lied.

After a moment, Hog said, "Piss outside."

I unbuttoned my trousers and pulled out my *khuy*, relieved that there was enough fluid left in my dehydrated body to redeem the lie. The wind instantly blew the urine back into us, and I heard Hog cursing. Somehow, I did not mind a little uric mist on me as long as it sprayed on him too. Comrades must share.

Hog said, "Now that you have soaked us both in piss, go back to sleep."

I nodded, buttoned up, and went back to lie down on the straw and wrap myself in blankets. They felt warm, even cozy, after the paralyzing cold at the door. I closed my eyes and drifted into memories.

"The whore," Stalin had called his mother, Ekaterina Georgiana Geladze. I could scarcely believe that Nadya would confide this to me as part of my research into the birth and youth of Joseph Stalin.

"The whore," Nadya hastened to say, "was much too harsh a judgment on a work-worn and exhausted woman who was repeatedly beaten by her husband." Nadya replaced the teacup on the saucer with a firm "click" for emphasis and set them down by the samovar.

"Ekaterina Georgiana," she said firmly, "gave sex to a wealthy doctor in order to keep her precious job as a domestic in the grandest house in Gori. It offered not only a stable income, pittance though it was, but the chance to steal food with her employer's wink and to filch good clothing that the wife no longer wore and never missed. Most importantly, there were the stolen blankets to protect herself and her husband against savage winters. You might say that she made a pact with the devil that she paid for by getting hell from her husband."

I asked, incredulously, "Are you sure you want all this in Stalin's biography?"

"Of course not," she snapped. "I am telling this to an intelligent man so you will better understand, and bring insight to, your biography of the greatest man of our time."

Nadya meant it, and I nodded. She offered me another slice of honey cake, which I accepted and nibbled between sips of hot tea as she talked.

"When Ekaterina became pregnant, the doctor's wife guessed the worst and screamed her into the street. She left the doctor's house in possession of two things: a small bag of coins he slipped to her and a fetus who would be born as Soso Djugashvili and grow up to become Joseph Stalin."

I asked, "How do you know that her husband was not the child's biological father?"

"Vissarion Ivanovich Djugashvili was a drunken cobbler who was so alcoholic that he could no longer manage an erection."

"How do you know that?"

"Ekaterina told me."

Surprised, I asked, "Is she still alive?"

Nadya nodded and lifted three photographs from a box and spread them out side by side on the table. "Look at these pictures. This is Soso as a ten-year-old boy, this is a photograph of the doctor, and this is a snapshot of Vissarion Ivanovich Djugashvili."

I could see that the boy bore an extraordinary facial resemblance to the philandering doctor. There was not the slightest physical or mental connection to the moronic-looking cobbler, who was drooling drunk when the picture was taken. Drunkard though the cobbler might be, the fact that he could not perform sexually meant that his putative son—who was not conceived by immaculate conception— had been conceived by another man. Vissarion surmised quite correctly that the good doctor had been humping his Ekaterina.

Nadya then showed me a photograph of a one-story, two-room hovel made of rough brick. "Abraham Lincoln was born in a log cabin. Joseph Stalin was born in this."

As I studied the photograph of the clumsy hutch with its shambling wooden lean-to garret, I thought, a person's beginnings could not be much humbler than this.

I said, "Tell me more," fascinated by the expression on Nadya's face. She seemed awed, transfigured, as if recounting a legend born in mists surrounding the origin of a god.

"The beatings of his mother continued through the birth and boyhood of Soso Djugashvili, and he heard the word *bastard* every day of his young life. Vissarion Ivanovich decided to get the boy out of his sight by apprenticing him to another tradesman. Ekaterina insisted that her son should get an education in a Russian theological seminary, the only chance for a poor boy to rise in the world. When she stood her ground, the cobbler beat her like a man insane. Joseph ran to the kitchen, found a knife, and threw it blade first at Vissarion."

"Shocked by the near miss," Nadya said, "the cobbler let go of Ekaterina's hair and turned on Joseph. The boy flung open the door of the hovel and fled for his life and hid for a few days with a kindly neighbor. Vissarion waited. When the boy finally returned, because he had no other place to stay, the cobbler alternately beat him and threw him against the wall of the hovel. In one such fling by the arm, he tore the ligaments in Joseph's arm and left him with a lifelong impairment. That's why he cradles that arm in his coat."

Nadya's eyes opened wide in anger. "Ekaterina heard his cries of pain and saw him writhe in agony. She grabbed a kitchen knife and joined the fray. Ekaterina put the point to Vissarion's throat and screamed that if he did not stop beating the boy, she would kill him in his sleep. There would be a throat slashed in the night, and that would be the bloody end of Vissarion Ivanovich Djugashvili! She would then take the boy and move away. The first anyone would know of his death would be the smell of his rotten corpse sickening the village."

"That did it," Nadya continued. "The cobbler stalked into his workshop and slammed the door. Ekaterina had sworn to kill him if he continued the beating, and she meant it. The cobbler could not break his spirit, and he could not break hers. Joseph the boy was already Stalin, 'man of steel.' And his mother, Ekaterina, was a woman of steel."

"Ekaterina dug up the long hidden bag of coins and dressed him in simple but good broadcloth to take him to the Tiflis Theological Seminary. Vissarion said nothing when Joseph appeared in a new suit and did not ask where the money came from to buy it. Relieved to at last get him out of sight, Vissarion had last words to Joseph: 'Good riddance, you little bastard.'"

"What became of the cobbler?" I asked.

"Killed in a knife fight, too drunk to defend himself."

"And Ekaterina?"

"She is still alive and living in Gori. Koba sends her money, and she still buries it. Once we brought her up here to the apartment, she looked around and said, 'This is very nice, Joseph, but what are you going to do if the Communists come back?'"

We both smiled and laughed.

I said, "Tell me about Stalin's education. I can scarcely believe he attended a religious seminary."

"Indeed he did. Joseph inherited the doctor's intellect and soaked up all the learning he was taught. He learned to read and write in Russian as well as in Georgian, and he loved literature. Almost immediately, he began to write poetry in both languages. Wonderful poems! Ekaterina's gifts of sex to a doctor were returned to her in the gift of a son with a high order of intellect in all things—who would become the greatest man of our time!"

I sighed as I admired Nadya's eyes, opened wide and glowing. "The greatest man of our time" was a mantra emblazoned on Nadya's soul, and it leaped from her mouth at every opportunity. Nevertheless, given the opportunity as Stalin's biographer to be near Nadya—to see her, sense her, catch whiffs of her fragrance, watch her elegant movements, and be aware of her body—I was willing, for a while, to hear "the greatest man of our time" one more time. And when this sensuous experience occurred in conjunction with work sessions that include caviar and eggs on black bread and triple-distilled potato vodka, what more could life offer in these times?

I asked, "What did he learn at the seminary that shaped him most as a man? Did he learn to love Jesus?"

Nadya smiled. "Gentle Jesus? Hardly. He learned to love Koba, the heroic guerrilla fighter for Georgian freedom and a very romantic figure. Koba the bold, the brave, the audacious. He became almost a god to Soso. From the time he learned of Koba in his youth, Joseph assumed his name as his own nickname and used it for revolutionary purposes until he assumed the name, 'Stalin, man of steel.' Joseph dreamed of becoming another Koba, a hero and a fighter as renowned as Koba himself. His face showed with pride when others called him Koba. How he dreamed of glory and doing great things for his people as Lincoln did for the Americans."

Nadya was quite nearsighted, and this led to a pattern of looking closely into my eyes when she talked—her face little more than a foot away—and her closeness and fragrance nearly drove me wild. Her honest innocence was erotic.

I managed to ask, "What else shaped him at the theological seminary?"

"He learned to hate the priests," she said.

"Why? Weren't they trying to help him?"

"Many reasons. Ekaterina had sent the last of the coins with him, and that's when he learned that the priests regularly searched the students' belongings—while they were in class—looking for revolutionary pamphlets. One of the priests found Koba's money and took it for 'the glory of God.' Joseph was enraged that his mother's hardscrabble savings had been stolen. Then it became obvious that the main lesson in every lecture was loyalty to the church and the Tsar, with some question of which came first."

Nadya continued, "Most importantly, Koba began to rebel against the humiliating regimen and the jesuitical methods. The basis of their treatment of the students was prying, spying, peering into the souls of the young people, so they had not a nook or cranny to call their own. Once they had gained insight into a student's inner self, he was subjected to endless petty torments to hurt his self-esteem and break down his will to resist the authority of the church. As Koba once said, 'What is the good of that? Does God want us to be mindless sheep being herded by priests?' When the bell rang for nine o'clock tea, they would go to the dining hall, and when they returned, they would find their belongings had been ransacked and turned upside down. This was intended to be humiliating, and it was. The physical and psychological abuse, in the name of God and the Tsar, did the spadework to instill a revolutionary spirit in Koba. His will was too strong to be broken, and he began to listen to the Marxist revolutionary students. When the rector expressed contempt for the growing Socialist movement, a student named Sylvester Jibladze arose from the student bench and punched the rector in the face—to the roaring applause of the other students. Jibladze had been Koba's mentor in Socialism, and when Jibladze was sentenced to three years in a military disciplinary corps, Koba stepped forward as the leader of the student Marxist group."

Nadya paused, then said, "Joseph began to read for himself the forbidden writings of Marx and Engels. He sought out revolutionary pamphlets and was soon committed to revolutionary Socialism. His antagonism toward the priests evolved into rude and insulting behavior. A priest named Dmitri came into Joseph's room while he was reading, and Joseph ignored him. The priest demanded, 'Don't you see who stands before you?' And Koba answered, 'I don't see anything but a black spot before my eyes.' The priest was enraged and filed charges of insolence with the seminary authorities."

Nadya smiled and said, "He was a handful of truculence. Joseph held study groups with other students until he had converted virtually all the students to Socialism. It was only a matter of time before the priests discovered what he was up to and expelled him for infidelity to Jesuit teachings. Their reasons for throwing him out were rudeness, religious infidelity, refusing to take examinations, and harboring dangerous views toward God and the Tsar. The real reason was his commitment to Socialism and the revolutionary overthrow of the Tsar and the rotten capitalist system. Joseph flew out of the seminary as a confident young man and a committed revolutionary for the Socialist cause. The Jesuits had done a fine job of making Joseph a literate and educated person and a fine job of alienating him from everything the priests represented."

Nadya was wearing down, and she concluded, "The young Koba went to Tiflis where he began to organize the railroad workers for a strike. And so he began his life as a revolutionary." She looked at me with tired eyes.

I asked, "Shall we continue another time?"

"There is something else I should bring up while I have the old photographs here." Nadya reached into the box and pulled out a picture of a lovely young woman lying in a casket. She said, "This is Ekaterina Svanidze, sister of another student in the seminary. Joseph met her, fell in love, and married her. They had a son named Yakov, who is now being raised by her parents."

I was startled when I saw the photograph of the pretty and voluptuous woman. She resembled the attractive young blonde who had run up to kiss Stalin at the Party Congress. Was he having an affair to relive his passion for his first wife? And then there were the love poems.

Nadya's eyes grew moist. "Joseph really loved her."

Fatigue disappeared from her eyes, and I saw something demonic: Nadya was jealous.

She hissed, "That peasant bitch took so much of his time that Lenin and Trotsky complained that he was not doing his revolutionary work. They told me about her—a real homebody without a brain in her head! They said she was a sex fiend who *poshol v pizdu* like a rabbit! She wanted it nine times a day, and Joseph did his best to oblige. She had breasts that would choke a horse. They said she was the best cook in Georgia, and she filled him with one delicious meal after another, seasoned just the way he liked them. They said he lost interest in revolutionary work, and all he wanted to do was eat and *poshol v pizdu!*"

I watched, fascinated, as Nadya worked herself into a jealous rage: cheeks flushed, fists clenched, hair shaking into strands. Very different from the composed Communist I knew.

"That ignorant peasant bitch adored him, worshipped him as if he were a god! She made his clothing, cleaned his boots, kept a house so clean one could eat off the floor. Whenever Joseph asked for something, she leaped to obey. Ekaterina Svanidze was a goddamn doormat for Koba, and he loved her for it!" She stopped as if choking on her fury, breathing heavily.

I could scarcely believe the ferocity of the jealousy Nadya was firing at the dead woman moldering in her grave, someone she had never met. I wondered if I dared to suggest this, but it was relevant to Nadya's fears and to Stalin's biography.

I said, "The love poems you showed me. Could they have been written for her?"

"That ignoramus was completely illiterate. She could not sign her own name and would not recognize it if she saw it. One does not write poems for a woman who could not read them!"

"Perhaps he read them to her," I said.

"Forget it!" she snapped. "Ekaterina had no interest in art, poetry, books, ideas, learning of any kind. She begged him to give up the revolution, take any kind of manual labor job, and live out his life with her as a pair of happy, stupid peasants. If he had read his poetry to her, she would have thought he had taken leave of his senses!"

The transformation of Nadya was breathtaking. She was possessed by jealousy to the point where I scarcely recognized her.

Nadya said grimly, "It was the interdiction of God—if he exists—that their marriage lasted only a year before she died, or his food and sex-addled brain might never have functioned again." Nadya quieted down, and she murmured, "At her funeral, I was told that Joseph wept like a child. A friend told me that, after Ekaterina was lowered into the ground, Koba turned and said, "That woman softened my stony heart. Now I have no feelings for any living thing. It is all so desolate inside. Utterly desolate."

I blurted, "If she had lived, everything might have turned out differently for Joseph Stalin."

"And for me," she said.

"And for history and the Soviet Union. You are right for him."

Nadya's eyes grew moist, and she stood before me, feeling diminished and ashamed. "I am sorry, Philip," she said. "I have made a spectacle of myself. The truth is that I have always known that Joseph does not love me with the passion he felt for Ekaterina Svanidze. It sometimes tears me apart when I think of it. Our love has passion in it, but it is mostly the passion of shared ideas and ideals." Nadya looked as if she would cry and said, "He never wrote a poem for me, not a single one," and hung her head down.

It was hard for me to believe that this svelte, intelligent, lovely woman would feel herself defeated by the huge mammaries and good cooking of a dead bovine peasant, but there it was.

Nadya looked worried. "Please don't put my ridiculous tantrum into writing. Please keep it as a secret between us."

"I promise," I said, and did not lie.

Nadya looked at me with drooping eyelids. "I am worn out. Can we work again another day?"

"Of course," I said, rising to my feet.

"But first," she murmured, drawing me down to whisper, "have you found the other woman?"

"No," I lied. "I don't think there is another woman," I lied again, thinking of the blond beauty with turquoise eyes and apple cheeks who had skipped up with heaving breasts to kiss Stalin.

Nadya looked through me with intuitive gaze and said, "You're lying to spare my feelings."

I lied harder. "When and if I find her, and know for certain that she is the one, I will tell you." I almost convinced myself of this falsehood, but not her.

"Who were the poems written for?" she whispered, her inner being waiting to be impaled.

I stood up again and changed the subject. I smiled. "Let's begin again another day, when you are rested."

Nadya smiled too and, to my surprise, took my hand to lead me to the door. She looked at me for a long moment with gentle, thoughtful eyes and said, "You're in love with me, aren't you?"

I nodded awkwardly, embarrassed.

"Does that mean I can trust you?"

"With your life," I said, and meant it.

Her expression dissolved into the elfin eyes and bitch-goddess smile of a woman toying with a man. "How do you know that I won't manipulate your feelings and use you for my own ends?"

"Please do." I grinned.

One laugh popped out, and she clapped a hand over her mouth, the ends of a smile showing on both sides and impish eyes over her fingers. Nadya giggled and said, "You're impossible."

Nadya reached up to cup my face in her hands. She pulled me down and stood on her toes to kiss me gently, with a brushing touch of her lips to mine. "You are a good man, Philip, and I know you will understand the kiss for what it means."

Nadya opened the door for me, and I stepped out onto clouds.

"Wait!" she blurted. She ran back to the table and scooped up half a fillet of salmon, a slice of honey cake, a hard-boiled egg and two slices of bread and wrapped them all in a napkin. She brought them to me with a smile and said, "Victor has probably worked up an appetite waiting."

I took the package and floated down the stairs and out the door to the street, thanking the powers-that-be for a writing assignment in paradise.

Victor started the engine of the car and pulled up before me at the curb.

I opened the door and handed him the package, saying, "A present from Comrade Nadya."

Victor opened the package, and an irrepressible smile spread over his face. He said, "I knew I had picked a winner," and bit off an end of hard-boiled egg. "Umm."

I entered the car on the passenger side, and he drove away toward my apartment. Victor looked sideways at me, repeatedly, as if sensing my euphoria, but drove in silence until we arrived.

I was opening the door to leave when he took hold of my arm and said, "Comrade Nadya is beautiful, charming, and good-hearted, but she is married. Please be careful about what you allow to happen with Stalin's wife."

9

> The young are the hope of everything,
> with eyes that glow and songs to sing.
> What futures can they hope to seed
> in nations fueled by gold and greed?
>
> —Joseph Stalin

I felt myself murmuring, at the edge of slumber, "I cannot get an interview with Stalin. He is always too busy to talk to me, and without interviews, I cannot get a sense of the man. If I do not understand him, I cannot write a meaningful biography. I am not a hack writer."

Nadya replied, "As Koba's biographer, you must spend a weekend with us in our dacha at Zubalovo and see the real Joseph Stalin."

"Wouldn't I be an intruder?"

"Poo," she said with a cute pucker. "You will become like one of the family. I insist that you come. Besides, we have an army of people visiting us on weekends during the summertime. Koba's friends and colleagues bring their families to party for two days and have a wonderful time in the country. You will almost be lost in the crowd, but you will see Koba as himself."

And so I visited the home that Nadya created and presided over, filled with the sounds of children's voices and the laughter of openhearted people. The names of the guests were then unknown to me, but here and there, I heard the names of Malenkov, Bukharin, Kirov, Molotov, and others—young troubadours and romantics of Socialism who dreamed great dreams for the future of mankind. Zubalovo, a dacha in the birch forest, was an uproar of important people and their families who showed up there as "the place to be" on a summer weekend.

Children shouted, played, ran, and jumped without being hushed, and Stalin watched them with slow grins, many chuckles, and an occasional outburst of laughter. The man of steel was almost excessively indulgent with children, and he gave them loud, moist kisses. Nadya was right. I was seeing a side of Stalin born of his own brutal miserable childhood. He had a soft spot.

Yet I found it no easier to interview Stalin at Zubalovo than in the Kremlin because, even here, he worked almost continuously. Little wood structures were scattered through the gardens and birch woods that surrounded the dacha, and Stalin would wander out to one or the other to read reports and documents. Some structures were nothing but raised wooden floors with a wicker chair and a table, some had roofs, and some were alcoves open to the sky but facing away from the house. I watched Stalin wander among them as if trying to find a place that was comfortable, always carrying something to read.

Twice I approached him for an interview, and twice he waved me away and began to peruse some official papers. Despite his evasions, I began to understand something about him. Joseph Stalin was a man alone even among his family and friends. Whenever he had a problem to think through, he withdrew even further and retreated to some place off-limits to anyone else.

His favorite spot was the west terrace of the dacha. It faced onto a garden where, in the afternoon sun, he could look at flowers, tomatoes, berries of all kinds on bushes, and apples and cherries on trees. I sensed that this was Stalin's kind of luxury and an expression of his peasant's love of nature and the soil. Once in a while, he would pick up pruning shears and snip a few twigs here and there, but mostly, he was content to look and let the brief interlude of summer feed the inner man. And he would think things through.

"You cannot disturb Koba at work," Nadya said, breaking into my reverie.

"Koba is always at work," I said with a little grump.

"Not always," she said with a smile.

A boy of seven and a girl of eight or so skipped up to us, yelling, "Mama! Mama! Mama!"

Nadya sank to her heels to embrace them. She smiled up at me and said, "These are my children, Vassily and Svetlana."

I solemnly shook hands with each of them as if they were adults. Children dislike being patronized by adults who use high falsetto voices to squeak down to them in pseudo baby talk.

Svetlana pouted. "Daddy won't play with us. He's working."

Nadya stood up and said, "Let's take a walk in the woods and see what we can find."

"Yay!" the children yelled.

Nadya said to me, "My soul is here. Look at how the afternoon sun has painted the grass and trees a buttery gold. Smell the fragrance of the earth. In the summer, there is the sweet heady scent of grass and, in winter, the wonderful tingle of cold and snow. An hour of roaming through the woods will leave you refreshed and ready to face any problem. I love it so that when my time comes, I want to be buried here among the birches of Zubalovo."

"Let's go!" Vassily yelled, tired of all this talk.

Nadya led the way down a path, followed by Vassily, Svetlana, and me bringing up the rear. Birds were chirping in the shrubbery, and sunlight steamed through the green dimness of the foliage. The rustle of birch leaves dancing in the wind was a kind of music. The enchantment moved us to silence, and I remembered the Slavic legend, "God lives in the forest."

There was sweet clover growing along the path, all yellow and white. Nadya crushed some blossoms in her hand and held them to the children's nostrils to enjoy the scent of honey.

We soon stopped in a meadow and sat on the trunk of a fallen tree. Vassily stood facing me, staring owlishly, and popped a thumb into his mouth.

I asked, "Would you like to learn how to weave a grass rope?"

Vassily nodded and took the thumb out of his mouth. Nadya and Svetlana looked interested.

I leaned down and broke off three stems of grass and held them between my thumb and forefingers. Then I plaited them left-over-right, right-over-left, center-over-right, and so on until there was a woven grass rope.

"I can't do that," Vassily said, impressed.

"Yes, you can," I answered. I plucked three more stems and placed them between Vassily's thumb and forefinger. Then I said, "Left-over-right."

Vassily pressed the stem over.

"Right-over-left."

Vassily bent the stem over.

"Now center-over-right."

Vassily did it.

"Repeat that," I said, "until you finish the rope."

Vassily panicked for a moment, then his brows furrowed in determination, and he systematically bent one stem over the other until they were woven all the way to the end. "I did it!" he trumpeted. He ran to his mother and shouted, "I did it all by myself!"

"How perfect!" she said, admiring the grass rope and glancing a smile at me.

We stood up. Svetlana took Nadya's hand, and surprisingly, Vassily took my hand. We wandered in silence for a while.

Then Svetlana pointed to a bird's nest in a birch tree. "Does it have babies in it?"

Nadya said, "It's too high to see."

"No, it isn't," I answered. I turned Svetlana around, facing away, placed my hands under her armpits, then lifted her, squealing up to the eye level of the nest.

"It's empty," she pouted, disappointed.

I lowered her to the ground and turned her around to face me. "We'll all come out here next year and look at it when the birds are nesting."

"We'll do that!" Svetlana chirped, brightening at the plan.

Nadya was looking at me as a woman looks at a man. "You're very good with the children."

"They are easy to like." I smiled.

"They certainly like you," she said.

I realized that the person I was coming to know at Zubalovo was not Joseph Stalin but Stalin's wife. Nadya had the seductive look of a young gypsy: dark luminous eyes that could stop a man's heart, a heart-shaped face with a turned-up nose that hinted at insolence, a full mouth that flowered from a pout to laughter in a flash of even white teeth. Her willowy figure moved like a ballerina, and I sensed the beauty of her breasts. There was something languid and oriental about her, something exotic. Nadya wore a Ukrainian shawl, white and scarlet, that was becoming to her dark skin. I was bewitched by her. She knew it, and I knew it.

The sun dropped behind the forest, and the air was soon chilled. Svetlana shivered, and Vassily wrapped his arms around himself.

Nadya took charge. "It's time to return to the others and think about dinner." She led the way, and we followed. I was deeply refreshed by this walk in the woods, an interlude of happiness so pure I knew it would glow in memory. Her last glance reminded me that the man who takes the hand of a child takes the heart of its mother.

We returned to a swirling tumult of people and party noises. The women were making clattery preparations for dinner, while the men were carrying wood into the fireplace and starting a fire. Teenagers selected records to play from Stalin's collection of Russian, Ukrainian, and Georgian folk songs, the music he cared passionately about. Vodka was poured, and the men told jokes and talked politics. Children fueled the uproar by getting in everyone's way.

Stalin came in quietly, poured a small glass of Georgian wine, rumpled the hair of Vassily, then walked out to the west terrace to sit and watch the stars emerge in the evening sky. I felt that this was the time to talk to Joseph Stalin—after the work and before the dinner—when he was open-minded. I walked toward the terrace.

"Philip!" Nadya called out.

I stopped and turned toward her.

"This is Koba's private time," she chided.

I was annoyed. When wasn't it private time for Joseph Stalin? How could I get a sense of the man to write his biography if there was never a time to talk to him? Stalin sat and sipped his Georgian wine, alone, and I left him alone.

"Philip," Nadya said, looking seriously at her husband sitting on the terrace. "Let me alert you to something important about Koba."

"What's that?"

"He is unforgiving. Though I love him, I know this about him. He takes things personally. If you take a stand against him on some issue he considers important, you will change instantly from being a friend to being an enemy in his eyes—and he will never forgive you. When you write his biography, remember that he is trying to lift Russia from being a nation of illiterate peasants to being the mightiest power in the world. His dreams surpass the visions of Peter the Great and Ivan the Terrible. Your biography must take into account that he is devoted to the people and everything he does and tries to do is in the best interests of the Soviet Union."

"I'll remember that," I said but bristled inwardly. Nobody could tell me what or how to write. I had a soul and a vision too, and at the heart of it was honest writing. But on the other hand, it behooved me to understand where my bread was buttered. The man who would shake the world could also destroy my world.

The buffet table was heavy under the weight of delicious food. At once, I salivated at the prospect of a wonderful meal and groaned a little to think of the millions of people living on bread and fat drippings. Only yesterday, I was one of them. The guests lined up to help themselves to meats, sausages, fish, salads, and cakes and searched for places to sit down.

Stalin liked sausages with potato salad and asparagus, and he piled his plate high before going to sit with Nadya on the couch before the crackling fire. Vassily and Svetlana sat cross-legged on the floor before their parents, plates on their laps. I made a mental note of this scene of domestic bliss for his biography.

I hung back and did not serve myself until all the others had taken the food they wanted. When I at last filled my plate, I found that all the places to sit down inside had been taken. I wandered outside to the west terrace to a table and wicker chair. The reports that Stalin had been reading were still smeared across the table. I moved them over to make room for my plate of food, and a small scrap of paper fell to the deck. I sat down on the chair, put my dinner on the table, and leaned down to pick up the scrap of paper. The paper had something written on it, and I held it up to the available light to read.

> There is only this one thing: To be the greatest man of the age, maker of legends and songs to sing and rise to dominion over all that lives on great and stalwart wings.
>
> —Joseph Stalin

I stiffened as I read it. This scribble revealed more about the true nature of Joseph Stalin than could any interview. This poem was not written by the savior of the Russian people, the Abraham Lincoln of the Soviet Union, but by an oriental despot who was committed to grasping for power. It was unbridled ambition for himself and his own glory. I returned the scribble to the pile of documents and thoughtfully ate my dinner. How could I write a biography praising someone as false as this man?

"Philip?" said a gentle voice

I looked up and saw Stalin standing there, leaning forward slightly, looking with kind eyes.

"Why are you sitting out here by yourself?" he asked.

Embarrassed, I stood up and replied, "I ate my dinner and then got lost in my thoughts."

Stalin wrapped his arm about my shoulders as if I were his brother and conducted me to the door, saying, "Dinner is over. Please come in and join the party." His warmth was sincere.

I heard the wild Russian folk music, the laughter, and someone strumming the *balalaika*.

Stalin released me and called out, "Nadya." He stood in the center of the room and began a heel-and-toe dance, clapping his hands and snapping his fingers. Everyone joined in, chanting, "Yah! Yah! Yah!" stamping their feet and clapping their hands and singing choruses at the tops of their lungs. Nadya floated out holding her shawl at arm's length sideways, like wings, and circled the dancing Stalin like a twirling bird—to resounding applause.

I could see that Stalin loved the dancing and the people he was with—these were the singing leaders of the new Soviet Union. People who like folk music and dancing cannot be all bad.

10

> Time has no edges, nor do we,
> weaving past into future
> with our loving and dreaming,
> we loom a fabric of eternity
> as the living thread the buried
> to the unborn.
>
> —Joseph Stalin

The train abruptly swerved as it was switched from one track to another. Hog and Squeaky tumbled across the floor to slam into the wall, grunting obscenities. I squirted out from under my blankets, and—gasping from the shock of needle-sharp wind and numbing cold—I snatched and scrambled to find my blankets and bundle up again.

"What are you doing?" Hog barked in the night.

"*Ni khuya,*" I answered, snuggled down, wide awake, and teeth chattering, waiting to warm up.

Nadya's figure took form in memory, carrying her textbooks, smiling apologetically to be attending school with students a decade younger. The hunger to learn was in her, and I realized that Nadya had a functioning brain as well as a mind of her own.

My research for Stalin's biography brought me many times to Stalin and Nadya's apartment. This visit was a surprise. The door was opened by a tall, straight, oily-looking man in his fifties, hair slicked thinly back, dressed in belted tunic, peasant trousers, and boots. The smirk on his face reminded me of a cartoon of an English butler in a great manor.

"Who are you?" I blurted.

"Pavel," he conceded. "I am retained by Comrade Stalin to meet the needs and protect the person of Stalin's wife."

Pavel looked down on me with the disdain of servants who work for the rich and powerful.

Nadya appeared at the door, eyes and mouth angry but fetching in a tailored maroon suit and dress boots, her black hair tied back with a red ribbon.

"Come in, Philip," she said.

Pavel stepped back to let me in and made the scarcely perceptible nod he would give a dog as I entered. He closed the door behind me and reluctantly took my greatcoat.

Another surprise hung on the wall. The painting of Jesus greeting the Russian people had been replaced by a picture of a steel mill with an open hearth cauldron and muscular workers heaving coal into the furnace fire.

"How homey," I said.

"That is part of Koba's new program to enlist artists to further the cause of Socialism."

"In one's living room?" I asked.

"Koba plans to have it everywhere."

"Have you ever seen the work of the modernists?" I asked. "Chagall, Kandinsky, Picasso, and others in the West?"

"I have," she said, "and I do not like it. I agree with Lenin, who said, 'Such art brings no joy to the working people.'"

"But," I argued, "it is an approach to the emotions and not necessarily to the mind. Did you have any feelings when you looked at it?"

"Yes. I felt like a spectator attending a circus sideshow to look at the freaks."

"Some people like it," I urged.

"Yes... Those who need to feel themselves elite and superior can talk themselves into liking anything that sets them apart from the ordinary. We in the Soviet Union believe that meaningless art is alien to life and irrelevant to Socialism."

Pavel stood there listening as if we were a threesome.

Nadya glared at him and pointed to a curtained corridor. "Do something useful," she snapped, "like make tea!"

Pavel stiffened, nodded slightly, and left for the kitchen.

She turned irritably to me. "Joseph has decided that since I am a student again, I should be a child again."

"Intelligent people learn for as long as they live." I smiled. "My compliments to the inquiring mind of Nadezhda Sergeevna Alliluyeva."

Nadya relaxed. "I hope you do not consider it silly that I, the mother of two children, should want to go back to school."

"It's not silly at all... But why? You are—"

"Stalin's wife," she said, completing my sentence.

"Yes, Stalin's wife. You have enormous power by just being his wife. Your wish is everyone's command."

Nadya looked at me modestly. "Philip, I have had very little formal education. I have not had any schooling since I was twelve or thirteen, and I married Koba when I was seventeen. Babies are not enough. I want to become someone on my own merits and not just exist as the extension of the great Joseph Stalin. If I can learn something useful and understand what is going on, I may be able to offer something worthwhile to the revolution."

"What does your husband think of all this?"

"Koba resents it. He wants me to stay home and raise Vassily and Svetlana. He calls educated women 'herrings with ideas.'"

"Being a mother can be an achievement," I urged.

Nadya looked acidly at me. "All I need to do to become a mother is to lie on my back with my legs apart. I have a brain, and I intend to use it."

"Don't your children need nurturing?"

"For heaven's sake, Philip! You sound like Koba! Are all men alike? I am here for my children until they leave for school, and I am here for them when they return from school. While they are in classes learning something, I want to be in classes learning something too."

"Good for you," I said, and meant it.

Pavel materialized, in his uncanny way, holding a tray of three cups, a pot of tea, and a dish of honey cakes. He put the tray down on a table, poured tea into three cups, and handed them out. Then he sat down on a chair to join us.

"Pavel," Nadya said with an edge, "take your tea into the kitchen and drink it there. We have matters to discuss that are none of your business."

Pavel stood up with lips pursed. He carried his tea to the corridor, pulled the curtain across, and walked stiffly to the kitchen to close the door behind him with a little less than a slam.

I glanced after him. "Why is he here? What a nuisance."

Nadya arched an eyebrow. "Koba says that there was an attempt to assassinate him, and he says that he retained Pavel to protect me... He says."

"If it's your safety he worries about, posting Pavel outside the apartment door should be good enough. Given the way he makes his presence felt, having him inside is really an invasion of your privacy."

Nadya leaned close to whisper. "I think Koba is a bit nervous about how often we see each other to work on his biography."

"You mean, Pavel is here as a chaperone?"

Nadya laughed in a voice like chimes. "Have you ever heard of anything more foolish? Men are so silly about their wives."

I smiled my sweetest liar's smile, seeming to agree, but it did not seem silly to me. Stalin was a middle-aged man married to a much younger woman—a lovely woman—and he understood that younger men would come sniffing around. I understood because I was sniffing around too.

Nadya suddenly stared at the bottom of the curtain where, in the shadows, the toes of two black boots were. Pavel.

She whispered, "Keep talking," and arose to slip silently toward the curtain.

"Well," I said in a voice to be heard, "Comrade Stalin's concerns may be justified."

Nadya raised her booted foot and smashed down her heel as hard as she could on the toes of one of his boots.

"*Ah!*" Pavel gasped and stumbled back.

Nadya yanked back the curtain and glared at Pavel, drooping over his throbbing toes.

"Sorry," Pavel murmured, shamefaced.

"You are not as sorry as you are going to be!" She pointed to the front door. "You are not welcome in my home—get out!"

Pavel turned up his palms, alarmed. "Comrade Stalin has assigned me to be here with you."

"To pry and snoop!"

"To protect you," Pavel insisted.

"Fine," she said, striding crisply to open the door. "Post yourself outside the door and don't come in unless I scream for you."

"But—"

"Out!"

Pavel shambled out, and Nadya fiercely closed the door behind him. She smiled impishly and walked quietly over to sit beside me on the couch.

"Wasn't that fun?" she whispered.

"Fun it was." I grinned.

"That should settle it for a while," she said, "until he thinks of another angle. The heart of the problem here—and this is *not* for publication—is that Koba sees enemies everywhere. He regards as sure only what he holds in his fist. Everyone beyond his control is a potential enemy. Koba views a world in which there is no choice but victory or death, and he plans every move in life like a battlefield general. Until he sees what you have written about him, you will be under a cloud of suspicion. Until he knows for certain that there is nothing intimate between us, I will be under suspicion. If my husband had his way, I would be locked in a palace with the children and guarded by a battalion of eunuchs."

"Have you ever given him reason to…?"

"Not once. Not ever. I am fully aware that I am Stalin's wife. Nevertheless, I think he feels uneasy that his wife is spending so much time with a much younger man." She smiled archly and murmured, "A very handsome younger man."

My invisible antennae popped up.

Nadya smiled sensuously and leaned forward to lay her hand on mine, meshing our fingers. "But you know and I know, and Koba should know, that he has nothing to fear in trusting Stalin's wife with you."

Was she turning me on for the fun of it? Nadya is either a *khuya*-teaser, or a woman saying, "Yes I like you, but nothing can ever come of it." Nadya announced she was *nev 'yebenno*, unavailable for sex, but then she played games that suggested the opposite. I was not into games.

Nadya switched out of her flirting mode and turned to pull a history book out from a stack of textbooks lying on a table.

"Is that for Stalin's biography?" I asked.

"I hope you don't mind, but today, I have something else to think about. My teacher, Professor Topol, has assigned a term paper on the value of digging a canal between the Baltic Sea and the Arctic Sea for naval and trade purposes."

"What a thrilling subject," I commented.

"This is another new project Koba is starting up. He has sent out orders to build public support for it, especially in the universities. Professor Topol wrinkles his nose at the idea because a canal in the Arctic would be frozen over and unusable for half the year."

"Professor Topol is right, but he should be more careful about what he says. The canal is not a new idea," I said, my historian soul leaping up. "Peter the Great began the canal in the seventeen hundreds but eventually gave it up because granite boulders in the soil of Karelia made hand-digging and excavating virtually impossible. It might be achievable today with machinery like jackhammers and bulldozers."

I then slipped into the role of professor without a ripple. "When you write your paper, begin with Peter the Great's realization that a sea voyage from the Baltic to the White Sea meant a month's sailing around Scandinavia. A canal would shorten the voyage to a matter of days. Then you explain why his attempt failed and why Stalin's attempt will succeed because of the use of modem machinery. You conclude by describing how the Soviet Union will benefit from the great vision of Joseph Stalin. I am sure that Topol will be fair-minded and bestow an A on the paper of Stalin's wife."

"That is pretty much what I have already written," she said wryly.

"Oh," I said, coloring up a little.

Nadya looked at me with cool eyes. "I want an A on the paper because it deserves an A, not because I am Stalin's wife. Besides, Professor Topol does not know who I am. The driver drops me off a distance from my classes, and he only sees me walking across campus like other students."

"I respect you for that."

Nadya looked embarrassed. "I have already written the paper pretty much the way you suggested. May I ask you to proofread it for errors?"

"Of course."

She handed me a folder with the paper inside.

I opened it and began to read. After a moment, I said, "Give me a pencil."

She gave me one, then sat there with a worried expression.

I began to circle misspelled words and grammatical errors and to balloon ideas that should be transposed elsewhere. She had come up with better concepts than I had realized, and my corrections were essentially editorial. Her lack of formal education showed, but her thoughts were sharp and clear. I handed the paper back to her, saying, "That's pretty good."

Nadya's face turned crimson when she saw all the corrections.

"Don't be embarrassed," I said. "You came up with good ideas of your own, you wrote them well, and my input was minor stuff."

"May I ask you to proofread it again after I revise it? I can give you things about Koba to look at while you wait."

"My pleasure," I said.

Nadya brought a box of photographs and papers for me to look through, then took her term paper to the kitchen table to rewrite. She was a darling woman, seated at the table with her brows furrowed, as she carefully wrote another draft of her paper. She was serious about it.

I leafed through the contents of the box and studied photographs of Stalin at different stages of his life: police mug shots when he was arrested by the *Okhrana*, the Tsarist secret police; several snapshots of him exiled in Siberia, including photos of him hugging a malamute dog he was fond of, holding a stringer of fish beside a lake, and standing proudly beside a deer carcass hung from the eaves of a log cabin. He had hated being exiled and away from the political action, but the wilderness clearly resonated in the soul of Joseph Stalin Most touching of all was a photograph showing Stalin and Nadya seated together on a grassy bank that evoked memories of sunny days at Zubalovo.

"Here it is," Nadya said, breaking my reverie.

I took her term paper and reread it. She had corrected all the spelling and grammatical errors, made transpositions, and improved her writing style. She had added new ideas that went beyond my suggestions.

"Well?" she asked.

"Excellent," I answered.

"Thank you," she said, pleased and a little proud.

"When is the paper due?"

"Today, in class. Do you think Victor would mind dropping me off at the university campus?"

"Not at all," I said. "I want to see it too and dream of the day I will teach at a university."

She kissed her forefingers and transferred the kiss to my lips. Games. We each put on our greatcoats to face the winter cold, with camaraderie and smiles, and walked out the door.

Pavel snapped to attention with hostile eyes. He had been brooding over his humiliation, and he announced, "I must come with you."

"No!" Nadya snapped. "You will stay here until I return."

"Comrade Stalin ordered me to stay with you and protect you," Pavel insisted stubbornly.

"When I talk to my husband that order will be rescinded, and you will be out of my sight!"

"Very well… But until then, I am under orders to accompany you."

Nadya turned to me and said, "I suppose we will need to put up with this nonsense until I talk to my husband."

We walked together to the exit, and I could sense Pavel's cold gaze on my back as we stepped out into the frigid air of Moscow.

Alert as always, Victor started the engine of the car and pulled up before us. Victor seemed startled to see Pavel.

"To the university, Victor," I said.

"Pavel will sit up front with the driver, and Philip will sit in the back seat with me." Nadya's voice was that of Stalin's wife, commanding obedience.

Victor rolled knowing eyes at me and jerked his thumb toward the rear seat. Pavel climbed into exile up front, while I clambered into the rear to sit happily beside Nadya. The weather was gray and gloomy in the city, but an emotional sun was shining radiantly in our back seat.

Victor wheeled and veered and wended his way through the city toward the campus. Along the way, we saw the usual *bezprizorniye*, homeless ones, rummaging in garbage cans, reminding us of those who were not sipping hot tea and nibbling honey cakes. Then the massive buildings of the university came into view.

"Oh!" she exclaimed. "There is Professor Topol!"

I saw a short, heavyset man striding along with a briefcase in his hand and a *schlepki* on his head, with a mind-on-business attitude.

Nadya rolled down the window and called out, "Professor Topol!"

The professor stopped and stared wondering at the car pulling up to the curb.

Nadya patted my hand and said, "I want you to meet my teacher."

When the car stopped, she and I emerged for introductions.

Professor Topol smiled and was polite as we shook hands. He was short and plump, Mongol blood showing in his high cheekbones and slightly slanted eyes, with one cheek sunken and scarred as if by a saber cut. Under the fat, though, there moved a lively and astute man with alert and intelligent black eyes. He removed his *schlepki* during introductions to reveal a bald pate with a rim of hair in back from ear to ear.

"Philip Makharov?" he said, searching his memory. "The name is familiar. Did you have a book published recently?"

"The Bloody Sunday of 1905," I said, very pleased that he knew of it.

"Very good! Very good indeed! Possibly the definitive work written about that terrible day." Topol thrust his hand out a second time to shake it vigorously. "I would be very pleased if you would drop by my office to discuss your book."

"I will as soon as I can," I promised. Praise from Caesar was praise indeed. And who knew? A visit to his office might be a first step toward a teaching position at the university.

"Time for class!" Topol announced to Nadya. He covered his gleaming pate with his cap and waved goodbye as he strode off.

"Bye now." Nadya smiled and scurried to catch up with Professor Topol.

I watched the two of them walk away, talking and smiling, and I felt good inside. Nadya was so genuine and unpretentious. Many other women in her position would be slathered with cosmetics, festooned with jewelry, and swishing with fancy clothing. Not my Nadya. Her cheeks were clean and pink in the cold winter wind, there was no jewelry, and her clothing was as modest and quiet as her manner. There was not a vain bone in her body.

The car door slammed, and I saw Pavel emerge and walk quickly after Topol and Nadya. Pavel positioned himself at a discreet distance that kept them in view but did not make himself obvious and then kept pace as they walked toward class. An internal security agent, if I had ever seen one.

How I resented him for following my Nadya. Or to be more accurate, following Stalin's wife.

11

> Let those who dream
> and sing their songs
> share a dream with me.
> Rising now with hand in hand
> on wings of words and arts,
> lift our precious motherland
> to its future in our hearts.
>
> —Joseph Stalin

I rolled over in my blankets and doubled up into a fetal position, half-awake and half-asleep, to dream on and on. I believed in yesterday.

"After all," Nadya said firmly, "an initiative as bold and innovative as this belongs in the biography of Joseph Stalin."

Stalin had put out a call for known creative artists to attend a meeting in the studio of the State Cinema Institute. Although I protested that a historian did not belong among truly creative people, Nadya bullied and badgered me until I agreed to go with her to the meeting.

The State Cinema Institute seemed so bizarre that Nadya almost had to push me into the studio. I looked about, amazed, at cavernous ceilings with catwalks, huge lights mounted on stands and cables snaking across the floor, massive polished metal reflectors, half-painted sets on freestanding partitions the size of walls, cameras too large for one man to lift mounted on tripods or wheels, and editing tables for cutting films—tools to create a world of story make-believe.

"Who are all those people?" I asked, pointing to the hundreds of men and women milling around and talking to one another in small groups. Row of chairs faced a stage and podium, but only a few loners were seated.

"Creative people from all the arts," she said, "here to listen to Koba lecture on agitprop."

I glanced from group to group and sensed what they had in common. Each burned restlessly with a visceral flame: intense people with the troubled eyes of inner struggle. Anyone who cannot recognize a creative person is the kind who misses rainbows.

"Who is here? I asked, beginning to realize why Nadya had ordered me to show up for a presentation on "agitprop," whatever that meant.

Nadya said, "I know a few of them. Do you see the tall powerful-looking man with shaved head and burning eyes? That is Mayakovsky, the great poet of the revolution. Koba is mad about his poems and reads them aloud to me. Mayakovsky is talking to Osip Mandelstam and Anna Akhmatova, poets who are *not* as enthusiastic about the revolution as they should be. Just beyond them are two filmmakers, Eisenstein and Pudovkin, giants in the new medium of motion pictures. Over there by the wall, talking as if the end of the world is nigh, are the painters Gerasimov and Repin. Koba is absolutely lusting for a painting by Repin. Beside them, along the wall, is Meyerhold, the playwright and director, talking to some actors and actresses. Just to their left are Khachaturian, talking to a group of composers, and Pasternak—the 'Hermit Crab'—as Koba calls him, talking to several authors."

I noticed, tongue in cheek, that they were all in their own little worlds. "They are talking shop. Writers are complaining about editors and publishers who mutilate their books. Painters are grumbling about getting commissions and pleasing patrons. Filmmakers and dramatists are groaning about budget cuts and project approvals. Composers are grousing to composers about getting their music performed. And poets are bitching to poets about a lack of public appreciation for their poems"

"I think you're right." Nadya grinned. "Why don't you join the writers' group and form a school of literature?"

"A school of literature is two writers living in the same city who hate each other," I said.

Nadya laughed in a flash of pearly white teeth. "You're impossible." She smiled.

"Comrades! Your attention, please!"

We all turned as one to see a thin man with a large drooping moustache standing behind a podium set on the stage. He gestured with his hands for everyone to come forward and sit down. The artists shuffled forward as if they were under duress to find chairs for themselves from among the rows set up for them.

Then I noticed Stalin seated at the rear of the stage with Pavel beside him. Nadya's blast had forced Stalin to withdraw Pavel from his position as a squealer snooping on Nadya and me. Both of them were looking at us, and Pavel was whispering something into Stalin's ear.

"Who is standing at the podium?" I asked.

"Maxim Gorki, a writer," she whispered.

"Comrades!" Gorki said again, after everyone was seated. "We artists are gathered here at the request of Comrade Stalin to discuss what we can do to further the revolution and make our Soviet Union the model for workers the world over." As Gorki talked, he began to be intoxicated by the sound of his own words, and he droned on and on in the stentorian tone of those who feel that history was there, listening intently.

I tuned out, as I usually do in the presence of sermons, and found myself studying Stalin. He was dressed in the plainest of the plain: a marshal's uniform and soft boots, without any decoration except a gold star—the Order of Hero of the Soviet Union—pinned on the left side of his chest. He was in movement constantly as he sat there. He fondled his pipe, which bore the white dot of the English firm, Dunhill. He looked this way and that and fidgeted while he waited to speak. In his movements, there was nothing overtly artificial or posturing. Even at this distance, I could see in his yellow eyes a mixture of sternness and roguishness, like an uncle a family does not quite approve of but loves anyway.

Maxim Gorki ended his unending sermon when Stalin, having had enough of a tide of words, rose to his feet and cleared his throat.

Gorki stammered, "And now, our incomparable leader, Comrade Joseph Stalin." Gorki turned and applauded with complete servility.

We all leaped to our feet, and I applauded as shamelessly as everyone else.

Stalin walked commandingly to the podium and returned the applause politely. Then he gestured for silence, which happened as soon as he asked for it.

"Comrade artists," Stalin began, "you are invited here because we consider you the finest artists of the Soviet Union, the flowers of our nation."

Relief and smiles spread through the audience.

Stalin bowed slightly, smiled, and applauded them, and the audience rose to their feet to applaud his applause, then sat down again.

"Lenin's pledge that we will proceed to construct a Socialist state will proceed from this point with a maximum use of your creative talents."

Applause again, but subdued.

"Today we will begin the battle to modernize our motherland. First, there will be the industrialization of every aspect of Soviet life. Peasants' farms will be combined into huge agricultural factories in which land, livestock, and implements will be shared collectively, and those who work the soil will share equally in the harvest. And as Lenin said, those who do not work will not eat." He paused to let the implications sink in.

"The surpluses from collective fanning will be sold abroad to buy tractors for the farms and machinery for the factories. The Western nations are fifty to a hundred years ahead of us in technology, and we much catch up in ten years, or they will strangle our young Soviet Union."

Stalin paused again, then said, "To achieve these glorious goals, we must create something new—the Soviet man and the Soviet woman. Only if we have a nation of heroes willing to exert every effort and make every sacrifice can we create a Soviet Union strong enough to resist the attacks from the West. Trust me! The attacks will come! The capitalists know that we will not settle for less than a world in which every working man and woman has enough to eat, a home to live in, medical care, education for their children, wholesome recreation, and civilized care in their old age. Lives filled with art and culture. The capitalists know that for them to survive, they must destroy our Socialist experiment before it becomes too strong!"

I sat there almost breathless. Stalin was speaking without notes, and every word seemed to rise from his heart. Stalin gripped the podium from either side and said, soberly, "We are presently a nation of illiterate peasants and illiterate workers. Our farmers feel themselves to be part of the soil they till and have the most bourgeois mentalities imaginable because they have never lifted their eyes above their own land. Our factory workers are so ground down at their machinery, working themselves to exhaustion just to exist, that the vision of another kind of life in another kind of social order seems like a fantasy.

"We can change all that," Stalin continued, clenching his fist. "We are going to hold up before their eyes what life will be like for them and their children under Socialism. Your art will lead the way in transforming every worker and peasant into a Socialist man and woman. Your art will be the beacon that leads the people of the Soviet Union into a future of sharing through Socialism. You artists, and you alone, can offer a vision that will inspire the people to make the exertions and sacrifices necessary to achieve our production goals."

We all leaned back in a hush, the very air churning with Stalin's passion and vision.

Stalin lowered his voice and said with gravity, "I have therefore invited you dreamers here to commit your talents to the building of Socialism first in the Soviet Union, and then in the world."

I glanced at Nadya and saw her eyes rimmed with tears. I felt jealous.

"Every artist will be supported in his or her work, but the art produced must bring joy to the masses. The art created must be another step forward in the building of a new Socialist order."

Stalin clenched his fist. "Composers will write songs with melodies that workers can sing as they labor in the fields and factories. Poets will write the lyrics for those songs—words that will raise their spirits and provide raiment for their souls. Sculptors will create in bronze and stone the heroic figures of workers and peasants transforming the world. Dramatists will write plays and actors perform them to show the cruelties of capitalism and project the joys to come under Socialism. Painters will give visual forms to the dreams of the first five-year plan and feed the innermost souls of the people."

We were overwhelmed by his vision.

Stalin raised his clenched fist into the Communist salute and roared, "Let art bake bread for the motherland we all love!"

The audience was stunned, and I among them. Then we stood up in a roar of applause that went on and on and on. I could see that Stalin was so gratified that he forgot to applaud in return. This was the Koba whom Nadya loved. Koba the dreamer, the visionary, the warrior who would create a new world and be the savior of working people everywhere. This speech was a moment comparable to his oration at the funeral of Lenin. This was a turning point in history, and I would write it as such in Stalin's biography.

I glanced sideways at Nadya and felt inferior to Stalin. I wished that her bright eyes and tears of joy were for something I had done. She seemed transfigured as if by an epiphany.

The applause died down, and Stalin motioned for everyone to be seated.

"Comrades in art," Stalin said, "are there questions?"

Gerasimov the painter stood up and said, "I paint flowers. Where do I fit in?"

Smiles and chuckles rippled through the audience.

Stalin smiled gently. "Paint your flowers in the arms of working men and women, and paint the people as if they were flowers."

A round of applause for Stalin's gentle answer.

Mayakovsky the poet arose, radiating power and spirit, and said, "I write poems. Workers and peasants do not read poems. What can I do?"

Stalin smiled and said, "I read your poems. The intelligentsia of the Soviet Union and the world read your poems, and your work inspires *us* to greater efforts for Socialism."

Mayakovsky smiled shyly and murmured, "You are very kind, but I want to reach the workers and peasants too."

Stalin thought for a moment and then said, "You can write title cards for silent movies and slogans for posters."

Mayakovsky seemed disbelieving but said thank you and sat down.

I could see that making art break bread might be a problem in the real world.

Someone asked, "Where do we begin?"

Stalin began to delve into plans and ideas for them to create useful art. He did not mince words but spoke with wit and humor—a rough humor—but with finesse and understanding. He addressed each artist with the *vy* used by Russians when talking to close personal friends rather than the more formal pronoun *ty* used with strangers. Stalin was so lively that it was hard to perceive how much was real and how much was role-playing. He sized up people instantly and spoke with skill in dealing with them personally. He was warm, welcoming, and human.

I studied the man in action. He was in part "real" and in part an actor—as were so many great men and women. Pretense was so spontaneous in Stalin that he seemed to convince himself of the truth of what he was saying even as he said it, changing personality with each person and each topic like a chameleon. Stalin made jokes and jibes in the service of Socialism, winning over the artists through rough charm.

Someone sat in the empty seat beside me, and I glanced over at the cold eyes of Pavel.

Pavel whispered, "Comrade Stalin wishes to speak with you after the meeting is concluded."

I nodded, half anticipating a lecture from Stalin about my growing closeness with Nadya. It would need to be a gentle lecture with her beside me.

When the questions dwindled away, Stalin said, "Perhaps I should tell you about the first of our great projects, the building of a great canal between the Baltic Sea and the White Sea in the Arctic. This will be a shortcut for our merchant ships and our navy."

"And," he continued, "we have organized something new to carry out the work—a *gulag*. We are going to empty out the prisons of murderers, thieves, and capitalist reactionaries and put them to work for the first time in their lives building this canal. They will redeem their crimes by working for the betterment of the Soviet Union. Why should criminals live idly in prison while we provide them with food and shelter?"

Everyone applauded and nodded.

"Henceforth," Stalin said, "everyone who commits a crime against the people will expiate that crime by working for the people in a *gulag*."

Nodding heads in the audience.

"And now," Stalin declared, gripping the podium, "if any of you have art ideas you would like to propose here and now, please speak up."

A short, plump man stood up.

Stalin smiled and said, "Comrade Sergei Eisenstein—creator of the great film *Battleship Potemkin*."

Eisenstein flushed with pleasure at this recognition. "I propose to make a motion picture entitled *Then and Now* showing the transformation of the Soviet Union, in which 'Then' is now, and 'Now' is the future of our people."

Stalin grinned hugely and applauded. "Now—that's creative thinking!"

Another artist stood up and announced an idea, followed by another and then another until the studio was an uproar of creative people shouting their ideas and clamoring for attention.

Stalin raised his hands with a quieting gesture. "Comrades! Please form groups and organize yourselves like good Socialists.

Present your ideas in written proposals that we can evaluate and fund on the basis of the betterment of the working class. Remember—Socialist art must bake bread!"

Stalin had turned on all the artists, and the studio crackled with creativity and excitement. This was quite a change from the artists who had drearily dragged themselves to the meeting. Artists in every medium sought one another out and began excitedly to talk about new ideas.

All of them, I could see, were imbued with a sense of mission that rose above self-indulgence in their arts. What a triumph for Joseph Stalin! I committed to memory the excited melee of creativity to add to his biography.

Stalin moved from group to group and listened to the creative people—really listened—and made suggestions. He joked and directed sallies and thrusts with artists, grumbling cheerfully all the way, the most lovable of men.

He gradually made his way over to us. Pavel stepped back, and Nadya stepped forward to embrace her husband.

"Koba, darling!" she exclaimed. "You were absolutely wonderful!" She threw her arms about his neck and pulled him down for a fierce kiss.

Nearby artists grinned and applauded.

Stalin smiled with the sheepish grin of a husband who was pleased to know that he had impressed the most important person in his life—his wife. He seemed so human.

Then Stalin turned to me with eyes that became inscrutable.

"Well, Comrade Makharov," Stalin said. "What do you make of all this?"

"A great day for the future of the Soviet Union." I felt impressed and showed it.

"Thank you," he said. "Now, Comrade. What are you going to contribute?"

"I am working on your biography, and today's event will read very well."

"Ah," Stalin said. "A biography is a long-term project, especially since I am a fair distance from the grave."

"What do you suggest?" I sighed.

"As the editor of *Pravda,* I would like to assign you to write an article about the White Sea canal and report how useless criminals are being put to good use—for the people."

"Sounds interesting," I said, knowing this assignment would take me out of Moscow and up to the Arctic Circle at Belomorstroya—and away from Nadya.

Nadya took Stalin's arm and smiled, though with reservations. "Comrade Makharov will see things as they are at the *gulag* and report them truthfully for *Pravda.*"

"I can hardly wait," I said ruefully. I had an inner side that was strange and dark, and that side loomed up as I saw her with Joseph Stalin. His greatness was beyond what I could do, and something inside me felt diminished. My star would never shine as brightly as his, to Nadya.

Stalin glanced at his watch and asked, "What's for dinner tonight?"

"I don't know yet. I have a paper to finish for Professor Topol's class, but he has not shown up for the last two classes, and nobody seems to know where he is. I suppose I should do it anyway and hope he will be there... Philip proofreads and corrects my papers before I turn them in."

I wish she had not said that.

Stalin looked at me with annoyed eyes. "Edit her work quickly so the children and I will have something to eat this evening."

I squirmed and nodded uneasily.

Nadya let go of Stalin's arm and said, "We'll sit in the car and finish it. Then I will go home and see to dinner."

"Fine," Stalin said, but he did not look fine.

Nadya and I turned and walked to the entrance of the State Cinema Institute. I glanced back to see Pavel and Stalin looking after us, Pavel whispering something to the great man.

I walked to the car, wondering if this assignment was Pavel's idea. Of all the writers at *Pravda* to send to Belomorstroya, the frozen hellhole of the north, why me?

12

> The fruits of the earth
> are hung on trees
> by men as well as gods.
> Let us harvest them
> to meet our needs
> and hedge the terrible odds.
>
> —Joseph Stalin

The dream turned into a nightmare. I awakened with enormous relief to pitch darkness, glad to find myself "at home" in my railway car. The snoring of Hog and Squeak sawed the air. Then I remembered my trip to the north.

Victor offered me a small gift of vodka. "This will warm you on the trip to Belomorstroya."

I accepted it with a smile.

Nadya took an envelope out of her purse and slipped it into my pocket. She patted the pocket and said, "That is for you to enjoy with your vodka."

An inner voice said not to open the envelope now.

Nadya said, irritably, "Why on earth does Koba insist on sending you, of all people, to report on the new *gulag*? You have a biography to write."

The question remained unanswered as we stood on the railway platform, watching prisoners being herded into other railway cars by armed guards.

In time, the locomotive engineer tooted the whistle.

TO SOME ABSENT GOD

Victor shook my hand with a concerned expression. Nadya offered her hand and then pulled it back to give me, instead, a brief, impulsive hug. She would miss me, I could tell, and the scent of rose petals stayed with me as I mounted the steps of the railway car. I was surprised to find that I had the railway car all to myself. Whose doing was that? I went to the window where I saw Nadya and Victor on the platform, looking up. The train began to move, and Nadya skipped along the platform for a few steps. When she threw me a kiss, Victor turned away.

The train chugged out and gathered speed as it headed north. I looked around at the private car with its bed, desk, and cooking facilities. If Comrade Stalin had to send me to the end of the world, he was at least sending me in the comfort of a fat capitalist.

I remembered the envelope Nadya had given me. I took it from my pocket, opened it, and pulled out a photograph of Nadya. She was dressed in a white smock and cap, and I recognized the background as that happy place, Zubalovo. I was mildly surprised to find that she had cut the picture out from a larger photograph—which I remembered had included Joseph Stalin. She had cut out her husband to give me this. I had lived long enough to realize that when a woman gives her photograph to a man, she is saying, "Remember me." I returned the picture to the envelope and clipped it inside the shank of my boot, where I had once hidden Lenin's will.

The window drew me with its flashing images of Karelia in winter, a land roughened by prehistoric glaciers, its soil filled with granite and shales, sands and subsands, clays and subclays. The map of Karelia I had seen was alive with towns, factories, and settlements—all fiction. What I found were tundra bogs and forests sighing with pines and birch. Where charts indicated grain fields, rustling in the wind were undrained swamps. Where reports promised electricity for towns and villages, there were only clusters of dark hovels and brown bears sniffing around smoky garbage dumps. The wind and cold of the Karelian peninsula were numbing even to people inured to the hardships of the north. The earth was snow-drifted and as hard as brick. And here, in winter, men were now ordered to dig a canal deep enough and wide enough for ships to pass through. In Karelia, there was not a single month in winter without an overnight thaw, not a single month in summer without an overnight freeze. In this tumultuous weather, men were expected to pour cement for locks, dikes, and sluices, a near impossibility.

What a page of history the story of the White Sea canal would be. This historian was under a lucky star. Somebody up there was moving me like a chess piece to bear witness to the birth pangs of the new Soviet Union. I began to look forward to the job of doing research and the joy of writing the article for *Pravda*. Nadya and Stalin would be pleased.

The train rumbled to a halt in Belomorstroya. I watched from a window as railway cars that were loaded with prisoners now emptied out and men formed themselves into motley lines at the direction of armed guards. As they lined up, I saw clothing ranging from the most wretched peasants dressed in rags to groups of tribesmen in ethnic garb to elegant gentlemen dressed in fashionable attire. Quite a mixed bag of prisoners.

Two men in uniform were waiting for me as I emerged from the railway car and stepped down to the ground.

"Comrade Makharov?" asked a tall thirtyish young man with black hair. He had oily-looking eyes, like ripe olives, and seemed full of himself.

"Yes," I said, enjoying the feel of stable earth under my feet.

"I am Comrade Yagoda, of the educational wing of the internal security forces." He pointed to a graying overweight man with the matter-of-fact expression of an engineer. "This is Comrade Kagan, chief of production for the White Canal."

We shook hands politely. Then I pointed to the hundred or so men now arranged in straggling lines and asked, "Who are those people?"

"All the dregs and scum of the nation," Yagoda said. "Murderers and thieves, of course. There are also priests, speculators, all kinds of crooked businessmen. There are real aristocrats, real landowners, servants from the Tsar's court. Some are teachers sent here under Article 35 for spreading anti-Soviet lies. All are wreckers of the new order and enemies of the people. All will be reforged into new Socialist men while digging the White Sea canal."

Comrade Kagan smiled a little at the introduction of his favorite subject—the canal. He gestured toward an uncoupled railroad car standing on a siding. "Let's have lunch in our facility, and then we can explain what we are about for your article in *Pravda*."

His comment made it abundantly clear they had been briefed by Stalin.

We had a pleasant lunch of bread, ham, and salted herrings, washed down with generous pourings of vodka and toasts to the success of the White Sea canal.

Then my hosts got down to business.

Kagan led us into a small office at one end of the railroad car and sat us down for a presentation. A large topographical map of the Karelian peninsula had been tacked to the wall. Kagan pointed to the red line of the projected canal passing through blue rings, representing lakes, the red lines crossed in many places with black lines to represent locks, dams, and dikes.

Comrade Kagan was full of himself as he announced, "We regard this enterprise as a battle fought for the future of our Soviet Union. We must push preparations for a heroic advance to fulfill and overfulfill our production goals. Every participant must be ready for the advance, mobilized for heroic struggle to change nature. Every engineer must be 100 percent competent in planning and allocation of resources. Every mechanic must ensure 100 percent efficiency in machines, horses, and men. Daily production attacks will begin at zero hour of arrival at the site and victory achieved 100 percent by the end of the day."

Kagan, I realized, saw himself as Marshal Suvarov facing Napoleon at the Battle of Borodino.

"This is war for the motherland," Kagan trumpeted, "and nothing less than 100 percent victory is acceptable."

"Supposed somebody achieves only ninety percent?" I asked.

"Then that slacker will receive only ninety percent of his food rations. As Lenin said—"

"Those who do not work will not eat." I finished his sentence.

Kagan and Yagoda beamed approval.

Then Yagoda stood up and faced me with the fierce eyes of the true believer. He spoke, though, in the measured tones of an adult telling a child to put on his galoshes before going outside. "We tell all the prisoners, 'You have broken Soviet laws, and you must expiate your guilt by persistent hard work and a "reforged attitude."' If the working class—masters of this country—are suffering privations, then their enemies must work even harder to prove their loyalty to the new Socialist order."

He continued, "An important aspect of reforging these criminals is to make them understand what part of the work they are doing, why this work is being done, and what will happen when the whole construction is finished. This way, they understand that they are part of a great Socialist enterprise. Knowing this, they work more eagerly, in a more comradely spirit, and their productivity rises." Yagoda went on and on about reforging class enemies into Socialist heroes. These two clearly wanted to be featured in my article and appear more equal than others. The very appearance of Yagoda spoke of self-discipline, of strictness toward himself and toward others around him.

Yagoda concluded, "For the new order to work, there must be internal security forces in which mind and muscle are trained to carry out the will of the party. Oneness with the collective is everything."

Mentally, I agreed with his premise so long as it did not apply to me.

"You have made your points." I sighed, ready for a change from unrelenting propaganda. "Much of what you say will be included in the article, and you will be credited by name."

Kagan and Yagoda flashed happy smiles.

Very good!" Yagoda said. "Would you like to see the work of the *gulag?*"

"That is why I am here," I said.

Yagoda and I stood up and clambered down from the railway car, while Kagan returned to his engineering plans. I was surprised to see my railway car uncoupled and left behind.

Yagoda smiled and said, "This will take a couple of days, and we want you to be comfortable."

He took my arm, which I vaguely resented, and steered me toward a huge camp in the forest.

Except for the sage-green pines, Belomorstroya was a place of blown-up, hollowed-out, dug-up ground with patches of dirty snow. The camp was alive with noises and teeming with prisoners at labor. Inside the workshops, hammers beat anvils, and wheelbarrows were repaired. Outside, prisoners worked at chopping trees, hauling wood, building barracks, digging earth, and laying down planks for sidewalks. The influx of prisoners had been so great that many were living in tents erected around roaring bonfires until the barracks could be finished. Soldiers with rifles were posted everywhere, and no prisoner was outside the range of a bullet.

We came first to a bathhouse, made of logs, being heated for newly arrived prisoners. Thick clouds of smoke from green wood came out of the chimney, and steam hissed through the door. A film of ice covered the log bathhouse, which reflected, mirrorlike, a cold winter sun. The swollen doors swung on leather hinges, flapping softly, almost noiselessly. On one side, prison clothing was being unloaded from sleds and dropped in huge piles on the snow: woolen mittens, boots, felt overboots, trousers, and quilted sleeveless jackets. One set at a time was being brought in to each man.

On the other side, prisoners stood in long lines to enter the bathhouse, grouped by ethnicity. Jews with Jews, Uzbeks with Uzbeks, Tajiks with Tajiks, and so on. Each man went into the entrance, undressed, and entered the hot steam. Each man emerged in winter prison garb, smelling strongly and strangely of disinfectant, looking sad and homeless. Bundled from head to toe in the same identical clothing, they looked like clones of one another.

I gestured that I wanted to enter the bathhouse, and Yagoda nodded approval. I swung back the door and went in to look around. A dense human breath, warm and stagnant, filled the steamy air. A hot fire burned in the stove, the iron chimney covered with sparks and breathing a dark crimson heat. A naked man, squatting on his heels, was taking advantage of boiling water to make and drink tea. I began to steam up and lurched out again into a wall of cold.

"What's next?" I asked Yagoda, convinced that the workers would be clean and suitably dressed for winter.

"Let's look at the barracks," I said.

I turned and saw lines of log barracks, about twenty by sixty feet in size, being erected in streets cut from the forest. Over the entrance to each barracks was a red star swinging like a squirrel from a wire on the eaves. I went into a cabin and found it reeking of turpentine. Rows of double bunks lined the walls, and a stove with a chimney stood in the center. Not exactly living quarters at the Ritz, but better than a dirty prison cell. So far, I had good things to write about the *gulag*.

Everything was made of the Karelian pine that grew there, I noted. The timber is of a sage-green color, of unusual height for the Arctic, and incredibly tough. For the tough fingers of a peasant, the soft hands of a professional, the sensitive fingers of the intellectual, taking an ax to these trees would be brutal work. But better to have them do useful work than to do nothing.

The smell of fresh bread and cabbage soup brightened my eyes, and I followed my nose to find a kitchen with wide-open doors. The cook, dressed in a white coat, stirred the copper kettle with a large two-handed spoon, while assistants behind him chopped up cabbages for the soup.

"Would you like a taste?" Yagoda smiled.

I nodded.

Without a word, the cook scooped up some soup and handed it to me with a slice of bread.

I nibbled the bread and sipped soup from the bowl. "Not bad, not bad at all." It was not French *baguette* and onion soup with cheese, but it was tasty bread and hearty soup—another merit badge for the *gulag* in my article.

"Would you like to talk to a prisoner?" Yagoda asked. He gestured toward a prisoner about fifty feet away who was grooming a small hairy horse that was yoked to a wagon. The prisoner was smearing salve over its sides and withers and cleaning its hooves.

I walked over to the prisoner, who seemed to be waiting for us. The prisoner was a tall and strong person, unusually manly and vigorous, with a dark weather-beaten face. I asked him who he was and why he was here.

"I am Guri Rosenthal," he said in a tone that sounded rehearsed. "I have spent my life wandering here and abroad, in and out of prisons. I was a thief, a swindler, and an adventurer. I am grateful that they took me out of prison to work here. Through honest work, I am being reforged into a new man. Socialism has given me a new life, and I will devote my life to Socialism." He smiled a wry smile. "Work for the collective is like bird lime. You give it a finger, and it pulls you in."

His speech sounded as if it were written and rehearsed.

Yagoda smiled and asked, "Would you like to talk to the gang of workers lying down the plank sidewalk?"

"Of course," I said with a smile but with growing reservations.

The prisoners snapped to attention in the presence of Yagoda.

"Who do I talk to?" I asked.

Yagoda nodded to a prisoner, who stepped forward and seemed as big as a house.

"We are the 'Forward to October' shock brigade," he announced through a beard covered by hoar frost. "We, the shock workers, with our flaming enthusiasm, will fulfill and overfulfill our responsibilities in this heroic struggle to dig and build the White Sea canal."

This was a charade, I realized. He had been planted there to make a speech, probably written by Yagoda. Every prisoner I was led to interview would probably be the same.

I turned and looked Yagoda squarely in the eyes. "Would it be all right with you if I walked about alone to interview some of the prisoners?"

Yagoda's smile vanished, and he stared back with the eyes of a raptor. "Out of the question," he snapped. "The prisoners are murderers and thieves, criminals of the worst kind."

"I want to write an honest article for *Pravda*," I insisted.

"Interviewing prisoners alone is unthinkable! They are dangerous!"

"No more so than the ones I have just talked to."

"Impossible!" he shouted.

I reached into my greatcoat and took out my assignment documents. I held the signature of Joseph Stalin under his nose. "I have the authority to see and do as I see fit."

Yagoda stiffened, then clicked his heels and bowed from the waist. He turned around, military style, and walked crisply away.

I looked around again. About fifty feet away, a man was struggling with a long iron bar to pry a tree stump up from the ground. He was a stout man with bushy eyebrows and a shallow Caucasian cap on his head. I walked up to him and waited, but he did not stop or speak.

"May I speak to you?" I finally asked.

"If I talk to you without permission," he grunted, "I will end up dead."

Taken aback, I said, "Not if you look away when you speak. Why are you here?"

"I am here," he gritted, with his head down, "for giving honey to a priest. I had given him nothing at Easter, and he seemed hungry, so I gave him a frame of honey from my beehive. A *komsomol* girl was walking by, carrying water, when I gave it to him. She reported me, and I was sentenced to ten years as an enemy of the people. Now! Please go away!"

He moved the bar to another angle, struggled with the stump, and hissed, "Go!"

About a hundred feet away, I saw a thick man chopping at the trunk of a Karelian pine with considerable skill. He was bearded to the eyes and gripped his axe with fingers as thick as sausages. He was all bone and sinew.

I walked up to him and asked, "May I talk to you?"

"No!" he said between clenched teeth. "If I talk to you, my family will never see me again."

"It can't hurt to talk."

"It can kill to talk."

"Can I ask you one question?"

"If I can answer it without stopping."

"Why are you here?"

"Article 58 of the Penal Code." He managed another stroke. "I was sent here for eating wheat heads," *whack*, "in my own fields at night." *Thunk.*

"If it was your own grain field, why was it a crime to eat the grain?" I asked.

"My farm was taken for a new collective." *Whack.* "Now," he grunted, "get lost before someone reports me."

I glanced up and saw dozens of prisoners staring at us.

"Goddamn you!" he snarled. "Go!"

I turned away and tried my luck at talking to other individuals and groups and asked them why they were here. All of them turned their backs and would not answer. The fear was palpable. I wondered, Could I put this intimidation into an article for *Pravda*? What would Nadya say, and would she believe it? Did Stalin actually know of the terror here, or was it just the actions of the authorities at Belomorstroya acting on their own?

On a hunch, I spun around and caught a glimpse of Yagoda pulling back behind a log latrine. I muttered, "What have I done to these men?" I decided not to jeopardize any more prisoners by trying to talk to them. I strode back along the way I had come as if I had not seen Yagoda and passed the latrine without looking back.

Yagoda suddenly materialized at my side, scurrying to catch up, and said, "Did you get any more material for your article?" His mouth smiled, but his eyes did not.

"The prisoners would not say a thing," I lied.

"Criminals are like that, you know. Code of the underworld and all that."

I smiled my liar's smile. "I guess so. What's on our schedule for tomorrow?"

"You should be able to write the article based on what you have seen and heard," Yagoda said.

"I need to see the work being done on the canal itself."

"Very well, if you insist," Yagoda said with a hard edge to his voice, his face turning crimson. "I have decided that you should be spared nothing in knowing what is being invested in men and material in achieving the White Sea canal." Yagoda turned to me with ominous eyes as we walked and said, "We do not want you to leave without getting a shovelful of the truth."

I chuckled as he expected me to.

Yagoda walked me back to my railway car and smiled as I climbed the steps.

He said, "Your dinner will be brought to you. Is there anything special you would like?"

I grinned. "If we have a wishing game, I would like some vodka and a cigar."

Yagoda laughed in the first human expression I had seen on him. "Done!"

I climbed up into the railway car, heated, comfortable, civilized. I sat down at the desk in the corner and sharpened a pencil. My impressions of this new thing called a *gulag* began to flow on paper. I scribbled faster and faster, page after page, so absorbed that I was startled when I was interrupted.

"Your dinner, comrade." A prisoner in a white smock stood there holding a covered tray. A nod directed him toward the table, where he placed the tray and left.

I stood up and lifted the cover to find a dish of roasted grouse, wild rice, and vegetables. A feast. Beside it were a pint of vodka and a cup, cigar and matches, and clean utensils. The aroma reached my nostrils, and suddenly, I became ravenous. I sat down and devoured everything on the plate, even sucking the bones to get the last nuance of flavor. My standard of living had gone up hugely since I started working for Joseph Stalin. Then it was time for vodka and a cigar, time for reflection. I poured up a cup of vodka and lighted the cigar, then took out the photograph of Nadya. I sipped vodka and savored the smoke of a good cigar and enjoyed her loveliness.

She had cut her husband out of the photograph she had given me. As a writer, I knew I could talk myself into believing anything. Nevertheless, this gift of a photograph from which her husband had been pruned seemed to me to be intimately significant.

The stars and moon smiled at me through the window and invited me to step outside with vodka and cigar to enjoy a bit of sensory overload. I returned Nadya's photograph to the envelope in my boot and arose to walk to the door. When I gripped the handle, it would not turn. It was locked from the outside. Either I was being locked in, or the prisoners were being locked out, possibly both.

I strolled back to the desk and reviewed what was written about the *gulag*. Not bad. Fatigue then took hold of me, and I decided to go to bed early. The blanket on the bed was already folded back. I pulled off my boots and, on impulse, took out the photograph of Nadya and kissed her good night. Then I slipped under the blanket, fully clothed, and fell into a deep sleep.

Rap! Rap! Rap! I struggled up from oblivion to see a prisoner holding a white carbide lamp and a tray with hot tea and bread with cheese. He had been tapping on the window pane above me. It was still dark outside.

"Comrade Yagoda sends your breakfast and asks that you be ready in half an hour to go to the diggings of the canal," he said and scurried off.

"Thanks," I said, sitting up in bed with the tray beside me. I sipped wonderful hot tea after he left and munched through the bread and cheese. My spirits rose. I put on my boots and greatcoat and found the railway car door now unlocked. Outside, I found a northern "white light." Snow had fallen, and the illumination was almost brilliant enough to read my writings. The camp and the two railroad cars were a silvery gray and arched over with the black silhouettes of Karelian pines.

"Comrade Makharov!"

I saw the silhouette of Yagoda gesturing for me to accompany him. Shivering a little in corporeal cold, I followed him, boots scrunching in the snow, until I reached a mass of hundreds, perhaps a thousand men.

Prisoners stood in crowds, bearded to a man, shrouded in black tarpaulin coats with canvas wallets thrown over their shoulders. The mining tools in their wallets clinked morosely when they moved. The steam in the cold air from the breathing of so many people created a fog that turned the farther groups into silvery gray silhouettes. I stood near one prisoner who had kept his own clothing, and he had put on everything he had: a shirt, another one on top of it, a vest, a quilted waistcoat, and on top of that a sheepskin coat that smelled strongly of fat and home. He could waddle, and only waddle.

"Move out!" someone yelled distantly.

The phalanxes of prisoners began to move like a black mass in the night, their felt overboots crunching and squeaking in the snow. Hoar frost dropped from the pine branches above as the prisoners trudged through the snow, light dry twigs falling with a crackling sound.

I followed after them in silence, Yagoda trudging beside me. We followed the trail of the masses of prisoners until we smelled smoke, and then we emerged from the forests into the digging areas of the canal.

Fires were already burning on spaces cleared of snow to thaw the ground for digging. Fires smoldered in the trenches dug the previous day, branches crackling and white smoke coming from the juniper twigs. Smoke crawled over the snow, shimmered upward on our clothing, got into our eyes, and left bitterness in our mouths. The fires may have been burning all night to soften the ground.

There was not a jackhammer or a bulldozer or machinery of any kind in sight. As far as I could see, the men were going to dig the canal exactly in the way that had failed Peter the Great—with picks and shovels. A distant "boom" reminded me that Peter did not have dynamite.

Shovels crunched into the ground as daylight emerged with a cold sun. The soil was soft at first from the bonfires, but soon the shovels reached permafrost, and it was hard as stone. Chains of men worked in the trenches, showing black against the earth and snow. Granite boulders were split into carrying size by two-man teams, one holding the chisel with tongs, the other swinging a ten-pound sledgehammer. It was brutally hard work.

Yagoda and I stood around and watched for hours as, fire by fire, layer by layer, the prisoners worked without a break to exhaustion.

An old man suddenly sat down and let his shovel fall. He sat on a chunk of granite, closed his eyes, and swung his body back and forth to sing a Tajik song. Bearded like most of the prisoners but gray-colored, he had large fleshy lips all grooved and furrowed, a narrow forehead, yellow wrinkled hands, and a flabby neck. But his cheeks were crimson and sweaty.

Yagoda turned to a soldier and said, "There's a slacker here."

I studied the prisoner's cheeks and said, "He's a sick old man."

"He's a slacker," Yagoda said, "and the others need to see what happens to a slacker."

I stood disbelieving as the soldier unslung his rifle, took aim, and shot him through the head. The impact exploded his skull and rained fragments of bone and brains over the men around him.

"Drag him out," Yagoda ordered. The other prisoners put down their shovels and lifted the dead Tajik out of the ditch. "String him up, but do not waste the clothing."

Prisoners dragged the body to the foot of a large tree. They tied his feet together and tossed the coil of rope over a branch. Then they hoisted him up to eye level, upside down, and stripped off his quilted jacket and vest and hoisted him again farther up to hang like an animal carcass.

I said through clenched teeth, "Couldn't you at least bury him?"

"The ground is too hard to dig a grave," Yagoda said.

"It's not too hard to dig a canal!" I yelled.

"Contain yourself, Makharov," Yagoda said. "This is how we keep thousands of criminals under control with a handful of soldiers—fear! We will leave him there as an example to the others until spring, when the ground will be soft enough to dig a grave." Yagoda's expression was as unfeeling as granite but tinged with a satisfied smile.

"I may include this killing in my article," I said.

"Comrade Stalin may not like that. What happens at Belomor should stay at Belomor. These…men are, after all, criminals."

"A man who gives food to the hungry or eats wheat heads from his own fields is not a criminal."

"That is subjective reality," Yagoda said. "Objective reality is that men are needed to build this canal, and those who oppose the policies and practices of the party are criminals."

I wondered, *Am I being warned?*

"Comrade Makharov," Yagoda added quietly, "it is in your own vital interests that your article be politically correct."

I was being warned.

A blast in the distance spewed dirt and stones into the air.

"What's that?" I asked.

"The attack front of the canal digging. We send the worst of the worst criminals there."

"I want to see it for my article," I insisted, now bearing a grudge.

"The trees there bear strange fruit," Yagoda warned.

"I want to see it," I insisted.

Yagoda looked at me with a wry smile, then walked over to give a hard shove to the body of the strung-up old Tajik. The body swung heavily, like the pendulum in a grandfather clock, and he said, "Tick-tock, Tick-tock, Tick-tock." He turned and walked with a grim smile toward the blasting face.

I followed after him, glancing back at the body, swinging and turning.

The blasting face was at least two miles away. We followed zig-zags in the digging as it skirted the forest. After four turns in the canal, we began to see the strange fruit: dead men, strung up by their heels and stripped of their clothing. At first we saw one or two, then a half dozen, and then an orchard of fruit beyond counting.

Whenever we passed near a corpse, Yagoda would give a hard shove to send the carcass swinging and say, 'Tick-tock, Tick-tock."

I realized that Yagoda was trying to intimidate me. A thought crossed my paranoiac soul. Was this a warning from Stalin himself? Yagoda had known all about me when I arrived and had steered me to only those things he wanted me to see. I remembered that Pavel had been planted to chaperone Nadya and me. I stared back at the bizarre fruit swinging surrealistically from the trees and wondered if this was Stalin's warning to back away from Nadya.

I asked sarcastically, "Are all those frozen carcasses the bodies of slackers."

"Not all of them," Yagoda said, pointing toward the forests in the West. "Finland is only two or three days' hard march from here. Some of those bodies are criminals who attempted to evade their duties by running away to Finland but were caught. Others are those who stole food or took clothing from other prisoners or incorrigibles who refused to become new Socialist men."

Yagoda added, "There are many more trees from which to hang prisoners who deserve it."

I stared at the orchard of swinging frozen cadavers and wondered if this was to be the real fruit of the new Socialist order. The scene was as surrealistic as a painting by a madman.

A nearby blast nearly deafened us and showered us with stones and debris.

When a second blast came, we turned away and covered our heads with our arms. The prisoners hunched over their picks and shovels and let the debris rain down upon them.

A third blast was so huge that it seemed a volcano was erupting in a geyser of soil, stones, and boulders, leaving Yagoda and me cowering in fear of being hit by something big. Some of the prisoners were knocked to their knees by the force of the blast.

In the silence that followed, broken only by the patter of late-falling debris, a soldier walked over to the edge of the crater and looked inside. He yelled, "A prisoner is killed!"

Yagoda and I walked to the edge of the crater and saw a man's body lying facedown, half covered by rubble, his skull cracked open like a melon.

"Get him out of there!" Yagoda ordered.

I watched as other prisoners scrambled down the sides and lifted him, facedown, up the sides of the crater. Something about him seemed familiar. When the corpse was dragged up over the edge, the body fell over on its back.

"Topol!" I gasped, staring at the cut in his sunken cheek and the open senseless eyes. The brain that understood so much now oozed into the dirt, and the warm, generous spirit was gone.

"Do you know this criminal?" Yagoda asked suspiciously.

"Professor Topol. A brilliant and decent man."

"If Professor Topol was sent here, it was probably for the crime of spreading anti-Soviet lies. That makes him the worst kind of criminal."

I wondered who could have reported him. Surely not Nadya, unless she had said something innocently to Stalin over breakfast. Then I remembered Pavel. He had followed Topol and Nadya to the classroom. The dirty *khuya* had listened to Topol's lecture and turned him in to the internal security forces, the GPU.

"String him up," Yagoda ordered.

"No!" I yelled, facing him. "Topol will be buried *now* like the decent human being he was."

"He will be buried in the spring when the ground is soft enough to dig." Yagoda turned to two prisoners standing there and ordered, "String him up like the others." They each grabbed a foot and dragged Topol to the foot of a Karelian pine.

When I started after them, Yagoda grabbed my arm and held me back. He said, "For a very intelligent man, you are slow to catch on about some things."

I got the message but said nothing. Topol was hoisted up by the heels and hung there, his brain bulging out, turning slowly as he froze into solid meat.

Yagoda walked over to Topol's corpse and gave it a solid shove. As Topol swung back and forth at the end of the rope, Yagoda said, "Tick-tock, Tick-tock." And he grinned.

"I have had enough of your sadistic *pi' zdun!*" I yelled. "I want to return to Moscow—now!"

As the railroad car rocked back and forth on the return to Moscow, I wrote and wrote until my article about the new *gulag* and the digging of the White Sea canal was complete. Every word of it was true, whether Nadya and Stalin liked it or not.

13

> I climbed the mountain
> to where the wild lilacs grow.
> The leaves clapped with joy
> to applaud the prodigal's return
> and a lark sang its friendly persuasion.
>
> —Joseph Stalin

The *slam! slam! slam!* of the train rolling over dips in the track made by the thawing and freezing of permafrost awakened me again, but I wanted oblivion. Why should I be awake and miserable when I could transport myself through dreams to Nadya.

"Philip! How could you write such a thing!" Nadya screamed, waving my article.

I had given the article to Victor to bring to Stalin at *Pravda*. Victor read it and instead brought it to Nadya.

"This is slander against the Soviet Union! You can be sent to prison for writing this article! Are you out of your mind!" Nadya was trembling with emotion, her alarmed eyes opened wide.

"It's the truth," I said.

"It cannot be the truth!" she shrilled.

"They are killing innocent men at Belomorstroya."

"Criminals! Thieves and murderers!"

"Good people are being sent there for trumped-up reasons, just to get slave labor to work on the canal. Men are being imprisoned there for helping the hungry, for eating grain from their own fields, for speaking the truth. Men are being shot for sitting down when exhausted."

Nadya calmed down a little to rationalize. "The *gulag* system is just getting started. They are dealing with dangerous prisoners who have committed rape, robbery, and murder. Criminals need to be controlled."

"Does that include Professor Topol?"

Nadya's eyes rimmed with tears. "It cannot be so. It cannot be. Not Professor Topol, poor lamb."

"Professor Topol was sent to the blasting front because he was considered the worst of the worst criminals. He had said the canal would not be worth the cost in men and materials because it would be frozen over for half the year. For the crime of saying that, he was sent to do the most dangerous work—blasting. Topol was untrained and unsuitable for any such work. Now he is dead and strung up by the heels like an animal carcass." My words were flat and brutal.

"He could have refused to work," she murmured.

"Refused?" I said, growing angry. "If Topol had refused, he would have been shot like the old Tajik who was too sick and exhausted to work any more."

"Obviously," Nadya insisted, "this is the work of the authorities at Belomorstroya, and my husband knows nothing about it."

"Not obviously," I snapped, my ire rising.

"Then I will tell him myself," Nadya said.

Victor cut in, "No! No! No!"

"You stay out of this, you dirty *khuya!*" I shouted. "You brought the article to her! You brought her here!" Craziness came over me, and I lashed a right fist at Victor's face, and he ducked. I threw a left fist, and he ducked again. I flung a right fist once more, and he ducked under my arm to grab my testicles and give them a hard yank. I doubled up in agony and sank to my knees, then fell over on my side.

"Why did you do that?" I groaned, trying weakly to sit up.

"To get your attention," Victor said and squatted down beside me.

Nadya stepped to the other side and sank to her heels. When I looked at her, she slapped me in the face—*hard*. She said, "I did that to inform you that I will not put up with vile language in my presence... Is that understood?"

I nodded.

Victor sat back on his rump and crossed his legs. Nadya joined him by sitting down on her side, propped up by one arm. We were a cozy circle of people prepared to discuss a problem in common—me.

Nadya looked at Victor and asked, "Why did you say no to my telling Comrade Stalin of the brutality at the *gulag?*"

Victor spoke tactfully. "I would like to believe that Comrade Stalin knows nothing of what is happening there and would not approve if he knew. On the other hand, I am a driver who talks to other drivers of important people, and we know what is growing in this country. The internal security forces—the GPU—are arresting dissidents in the middle of the night, and they vanish without a trace."

"That does not mean Koba knows about it," she said defensively.

I announced, "Comrade Stalin will find out about it when he reads the article."

Victor leaned toward me and said, "Look, Comrade Cloud Dweller. If Stalin reads that article, you may well take Topol's place at the blasting face. You might end by being strung up by the heels until the ground is soft enough to bury you."

"Koba would never do such a thing!" she flared.

"Maybe not," Victor said, "but the people around him would. What Comrade Makharov has written should not be seen, let alone be published."

Angrily, I shouted, "Every word is true, and I will not change it!"

"Your life is at stake, and we cannot indulge you the luxury of suicide," Victor said.

Nadya leaned forward to lay her hand tenderly on my cheek. "Please, Philip. Change it."

"No," I said, Topol swinging in my mind.

"Please change it for me," she urged anxiously.

"No."

Suddenly, Nadya's eyes were frightened, and she shouted, "I won't be torn apart between Koba and you." Tears welled in her eyes. "Please, please do it for me! Do it for us!"

Migod, I thought. *Her heart is on her sleeve.*

Victor stared at her with knowing eyes.

We sat for what seemed an eternity in silence.

"What do you want me to change?" I said, not knowing what I had said until I heard my voice.

"Everything," she urged.

"Write a propaganda piece?"

"If need be."

"Lying would make me a literary whore," I grumbled.

Victor commented, "I have seen you lie frequently and skillfully. And without qualms, I might add. You should not be so precious about a lie that saves your life."

"What's all this to you!" I roared.

"We are friends," Victor said quietly. "I place a high premium on friendship, even with a chronic and pathological liar."

I stood up, thinking it over. Nadya and Victor rose to their feet as well.

"All right," I said, looking at Nadya. "I will do whatever you ask because it is you who asks."

Relief flooded their faces.

"What should I do? Tell me," I said, feeling like her slave.

"Start over fresh." Nadya smiled.

I groaned.

"Do not even look at your first article," she said, tossing it on the floor. "Start over with a fresh sheet of paper—now."

I looked away, ashamed. "Am I, cold sober, expected to write a pack of lies?"

Victor smiled and said, "Let's make a party of it." He picked up a package I had barely been aware he had brought in and opened it. He took out a bottle and said, "Your favorite, lemon vodka," and reached to the bottom of the bag to pull up cigars and matches.

I laughed, and Nadya smiled.

Victor walked over to the board that was my desk. He opened the bottle of vodka and filled the cup that was standing there.

Nadya turned on the light bulb, and for once, there was electricity.

"That's an omen," I said, sitting down to my desk to sip some vodka.

Nadya brought a pad of blank paper and set it before me. She took my penknife, sharpened some pencils, and also placed those before me.

Victor retrieved the penknife and sliced off an end of the cigar. He put the cigar into his mouth, lighted it, and placed it into my mouth.

"No excuses," Nadya said. "Write!"

"Come back in two hours, and it will be ready."

"No," she said. "We will wait for it."

"Don't you trust me?" I bleated.

Victor laughed a single loud guffaw.

Nadya said, "Not with this article, we don't."

"Why do you both need to be here?"

Nadya said, "I will proofread and edit your article, and Victor will bring it to *Pravda*."

I looked up incredulously at Nadya. "*You* will edit *my* writing?"

"If you can correct my papers, I can correct yours. It must be politically correct."

"You know that I hate writing under pressure," I snapped.

"Too bad," she said matter-of-factly. She stepped beside me, took the cigar out of my mouth, and leaned down to plant a smack on my lips. "Go to it," she said and put the cigar back into my mouth. She ran her fingers along the nape of my neck, then rumpled my hair.

I had to smile. Vodka, cigars, and seduction, just to make me write.

Victor said with a smile, "Put your mind to writing, my friend."

I nodded and stared at the blank page until words came. I wrote the first sentence and read it aloud: "Thanks to the genius of Joseph Stalin, the White Sea canal will vastly strengthen the Soviet Union and reforge criminals into heroes of the proletariat—Socialist men willing to sacrifice themselves for the future of the working class."

"Splendid!" Nadya said.

"Good start," Victor growled approvingly.

"A crock of *gavno*," I said.

"No vile language in my presence!" Nadya warned.

"Get on with it," Victor grumped.

I settled into writing the article, remembering Kagan's military words and context, Yagoda's so-called commitment to remaking criminals into Socialist men, and the nonsense prisoners recited when I questioned them. I wrote about good food and warm clothing, about the courage and eagerness of prisoners to work and reform themselves, all *pi'zdun*.

Occasionally, I would glance up, and Nadya glanced away. At other times, she held my gaze for a long moment before looking away. She pretended to browse through the books in my library, but she was watching me write. Victor walked around and sipped a little vodka.

Halfway through the bottle of vodka, the revised article was finished.

"Here it is," I said.

Nadya strode over and took the pages and began to read the article, smiling a little as she went, moving each page to the bottom as it was finished. She frowned a little and stopped. She leaned over and pointed to the word *propaganda*. She said, "Could we change that to *education?*"

I changed it.

Victor looked over her shoulder and said, "Perhaps we should play up the Socialist man angle."

"What is this," I growled, "a committee report?"

Nadya looked at me crisply. "We will be the final judges of what is published in *Pravda*."

"Jesus."

"Do not blaspheme! Do all writers curse over their work?"

"Yes."

And so it went, a word here and a phrase there, a changed concept and revised pages. I thought it would never end. I had never been through project editors as tough as these two.

Nadya read it one last time, passing each page to Victor as she read it. Then they were finished.

"A fine article for *Pravda*," she said.

"Politically perfect," Victor said.

"I feel like a whore," I said. "How can I look myself in the mirror to shave?"

"You do not shave anyway. You have a beard," Victor said.

"Your beard is red, curly, and adorable," she said.

"Cheer up!" Victor smiled. "Now you still have a life to live!"

I flared, "I am not afraid to send the first version to *Pravda*." Surprisingly—it was true.

Nadya ran her fingers through my hair and said, "Men are such fools. Always trying to prove something that means nothing."

Victor looked away, uncomfortable.

"Victor," Nadya said, "take the article and wait for me outside."

He took the manuscript and let himself out the door, closing it quietly.

I stood up to face her. She reached up to place a palm on each cheek and pulled down my head for a long, moist kiss on the lips.

"Thank you, Philip," she said. "You hated doing the article over, but you did it for me. And I hope that you realize that we did what we had to do, just in case, to protect your life. I want you to understand that Joseph Stalin—my Koba—had nothing to do with the brutality at the *gulag*. He is an idealist, a dreamer, so busy with his visions for the people that he cannot take the time to see how his ideas are carried out. Please understand that Joseph Stalin will become the Abraham Lincoln of the Soviet Union."

Nadya turned away and walked to the door. She looked back at me and said, "You cannot imagine the inner turmoil of a woman who loves two men at the same time."

Then she left me to silence. I sat down to the board that was my desk, dazed by the implications of what she had said. I picked up a pencil and began to write down my feelings for Nadya in a form that was strange to me: poetry.

> At the far boundary of a smile, near the last
> tone before silence, I stepped forth from aridity
> to welcome a shower of joy at seeing you again…

The words ran dry, and I stopped writing. I had sold out Topol and all the others, and I knew it. Seduced by love on the one hand and bullied by friendship on the other, I had sold out. The image of Topol strung up like an animal carcass swung before the eyes of my memory.

"Tick-tock, Tick-tock."

What kind of a new social order was it when one good man was killed for speaking the truth and another—if I was a good man—was unable to write the truth and stand by it? Nadya could melt me down like a lump of wax any time she showed her feelings for me. The weakness was mine.

The pencil fell from my fingers. I did not have the heart to write another word. I looked about the room, and my gaze fell upon the first version of the article, lying on the floor where Nadya had thrown it. I stood up, retrieved the article, and reread it under the light bulb. Every word of it burned with the truth. This could not be thrown away. There might come a time when the truth had its place in the sun.

I looked around for a place to hide it and saw the box of papers holding Stalin's biography. The irony of putting the truth into a box of lies was not lost on me. I pulled back the top papers and slipped it underneath. As I stood up, I felt somehow bereft and lost.

Dirty is the word to describe my feelings. I went into the bathroom to wash my hands and glanced into the mirror to see a red-bearded, red-haired face with bleary eyes. The face of a spineless weakling.

"Whore!" I yelled. "You whore!"

14

> I cannot walk away
> from the weight
> upon my footsteps,
> nor leave the shadow
> of my corporeal form
> cast upon the ground.
> My shadow, and scheming,
> are with me always.
>
> —Joseph Stalin

The shriek of railroad brakes awakened me for a moment to see a glimpse of the false dawn, like a nocturnal painting by Repin. Then I drifted away again into dreams.

"You cannot go to dinner at the Voroshilovs dressed like that," Nadya said, pointing to my shabby tunic belted in over threadbare trousers thrust into shabby boots worn down at the heels.

"Why invite me to dinner at the Voroshilovs at all?" I asked.

"An important American writer and publisher will be there. Max Eastman is a Socialist comrade who publishes *New Masses* magazine in the United States and Koba wants to use him to present to the American people what we are trying to achieve in the Soviet Union. He especially wants you to make a writer's connection with Eastman so you can funnel propaganda to his magazine and try to offset some of the hostility we are getting in the American press."

I thought of Trotsky's remark; Stalin doesn't miss a trick.

"And," Nadya added, "there is something else. Max Eastman was the editor who sent John Reed to Russia to report on the revolution. Reed wrote the famous book *Ten Days that Shook the World*, then died of cholera and was buried within the walls of the Kremlin as a hero of the Soviet Union."

"What's the problem?" I asked.

"Eastman has been making inquiries among those who knew Reed in Russia about the circumstances surrounding his death. It was all quite innocent—and tragic—but Koba is anxious to put his mind at ease about the death of John Reed."

If Trotsky's words were true, Stalin had Reed murdered to shut him up. But I said nothing.

"Now," she said. "Let's buy some clothing that will make you presentable as the distinguished biographer of Joseph Stalin." She ordered Victor to drive us to a building on Granovsky Street that seemed from the outside to be a prison, though the people entering and leaving it were dressed in the most fashionable clothing. Nadya showed her identification card to the guard, who leaped to open the door for us.

When I entered the brilliantly illuminated building, I could scarcely believe my eyes: racks of elegant imported clothing, walls displaying fine Italian boots and shoes, cases of rare French wines and cognacs, and bins of oranges and bananas and produce that money could not buy outside these walls, with kiosks for barbers, tailors, and custom shoemakers.

The words popped out of my mouth in a flash of anger. "Is all this luxury for the few consistent with the high ideals of Socialism? People are living like dirty dogs in the street."

Nadya snapped, "Stalin said that every Leninist knows—every real Leninist—that equality in the sphere of requirements and individual life is a piece of reactionary petty bourgeois absurdity. If Stalin says it is so, it is so. Now shut your petty bourgeois mouth and let me make you presentable for a party of very important people at the Voroshilovs."

I shut up and followed her like a sheep.

Nadya took me first to the barber and said, "Shave and haircut." I arose, feeling naked.

That done, Nadya dressed me and personally picked what I should wear for this splendid occasion: a white Ukrainian tunic with high stitched collar and red embroidery running down the left side of the chest, fresh new trousers that were elegant under an Italian leather belt and tucked into shiny new boots as soft as glove leather. Nadya looked at everything with practiced eyes and ran her hands over my chest and shoulders to feel the fit while I enjoyed her fragrance. She sank to her heels and ran her hands down my trouser legs, then looked up at me with knowing eyes and the edges of a smile when my *khuy* responded to all this touching.

Then she stood up and said, "Look at yourself in the mirror."

I almost gasped—I had never looked so magnificent in my life. I was glorious!

Nadya said, "I won't spoil this by telling you how handsome you are."

For a long moment, I could not take my eyes off me.

"Time for you to return to being a caterpillar," she said. I packed my new clothing and put on the old rags, feeling like a gigolo as Nadya paid for everything.

I walked over to the produce section and selected a dozen oranges and paid an astronomical sum for them. Nadya looked at me with questioning eyes, and I said, "For Victor."

She nodded approvingly.

We walked out of the building into a wall of incredible cold. An old *babushka* stood at the curb, her head down and gnarled hands hanging at her side. She was too proud to beg, but she was begging. I reached into the bag and took out two oranges and offered them to her. She snatched them and looked up with moist old eyes, crossed herself, and started to kneel. Embarrassed, I lifted her elbow and waved away her thanks.

Nadya glanced sideways at me and said, "You are so human, Philip."

Compliments make me uncomfortable, but I smiled my thanks instead of squirming.

Nadya said, "Tonight at the Voroshilovs."

That evening, Victor drove me to the Voroshilov residence in a yellow-brick apartment building on Alexei Tolstoy Street. Two guards stood in sentry boxes; a *dezhurnaye*, a duty-woman, was present to open the door to the building. Posh for the Bolshevik scene.

The first surprise of the evening came as I clambered out of the car. Stepping out from a party limousine was the little blond beauty I had seen kissing Stalin. Showing up here was real *chutzpah!* Helping her out of the car was a tall, slender man with a leonine shock of blond hair and bright-blue eyes, dressed in a tweed jacket and tie and rumpled trousers. He looked like a literature professor. She took his arm and smiled up at him as if he were a lover. Was she a courtesan?

As a guest of the Voroshilovs, invited by Stalin, I sailed through the entrance without question.

Klim Voroshilov opened the door to the suite himself and revealed a home ablaze with lights, luxury, and important people. Voroshilov had the look of a noncommissioned officer: big, lanky, and commanding, but with a broad smile that all but split his head.

I stood back and let the tall foreigner and his lady of the evening go first. He introduced himself as Max Eastman—in excellent Russian—and the diminutive doll as Eliena Krylenko.

I perked up. Eliena Krylenko? Sister of the famed guerrilla fighter Georgi Krylenko? Secretary to the first foreign minister of the Soviet Union? She looked no more than seventeen: a girl, a flower.

Eliena Krylenko apparently knew Klim Voroshilov and gave him a big hug and a kiss, which I rather envied. Then she entered, and I saw her scurry over to give a hug and a kiss to Joseph Stalin in front of Nadya. I realized that she could not be the love interest expressed in Stalin's poems. Giving a monsoon of clutchy hugs and showering kisses were her way of saying hello.

I looked around the dining room. Migod, what a spread! The banquet tables groaned with delicacies: smoked salmon, several kinds of caviar, roast suckling pig, and a cut haunch of rare beef. The *zakuski* table sagged with its dishes of hors d'oeuvres: marinated mushrooms, salted herrings, salami, pickled cucumbers, caviar and eggs on crackers, cold tongue, red beet salad, scallions, and on and on. Bottles of triple distilled Polish vodka lined the back of the *zakuski* table, with rows of tumblers so the delicacies could be washed down with the very best vodka. On every flat surface were dishes of *vobla*, a dried and salted fish that one could crunch like potato chips. Waiters in white livery passed hot snacks and vodka, while a small stringed orchestra played frisky Russian folk songs, and a baritone filled the room with his voice.

This was truly *lyuks*—luxury—for these desperate times.

I quietly drifted along the edges of the party in search of a secluded alcove from which to view the scene, grateful that Nadya had dressed me properly for this sumptuous occasion. I would otherwise have been taken for a beggar who had somehow slipped into the event.

Stalin made a point of personally introducing Max Eastman to the guests and their wives: Zinoviev, the former actor who never stopped talking; Kamenev, the academic who looked as if he slept in his clothes; followed by so many talking and laughing *apparatchiks* and *nomenklatura* that one lost track of their names.

And then there was Lavrentiy Beria, a balding man of enameled composure, who stared with unblinking eyes through wire-rimmed glasses at the women present.

Stalin saw me huddled at the edge of the party, trying not to be noticed, and he waved me over. "Two fine writers should know each other!" he called.

I wended my way over to the *zakuski* table and shook hands with Max Eastman. I liked his modest and unassuming manner and the twinkle of humor latent in his eyes. He had *skirokaya dusha*, openness of spirit. There was no guile in him—like Trotsky—just high intelligence and a fair-minded attitude. Much taller, though, than the rest of us.

Stalin looked at Eastman with a challenging smile. "I want to see if I can trust you," he said. He stood up two tumblers and filled them to the top with vodka.

Eliena blurted, "Don't do it, Max. He's trying to make you drunk."

Max smiled and said to Stalin, "Back home, we do this with bourbon."

Stalin picked up a tumbler and drank the vodka, neat, then whacked the glass down.

Max took his tumbler, eyed it skeptically for a moment, then downed the vodka and slammed the glass on the table.

Applause erupted around the room, and Stalin shouted, "I can trust Max Eastman! A Socialist from the wrong side of the ocean, but very much a man!" Then Stalin took Eastman by the arm and began to build a bond of friendship by talking shop: the editor of *Pravda* with the editor of *New Masses* magazine. Very cozy.

"Do you like the party?" Nadya materialized beside me dressed exquisitely in vermilion silk brocade imported from another planet.

"Far grander than I imagined," I said and smiled. "Red becomes you."

She curtsied quietly and murmured, "Thank you." Then her eyes went cold, and she said, "How dare you look at Stalin's wife, you grub!"

I glanced over and saw Beria looking her over through his wire-rimmed glasses.

Nadya stared back just as rudely and said, "I hear bad things about Lavrentiy Beria."

"What bad things?"

"They say he goes hunting for young women in a special car, then rapes them."

"Why does Stalin keep him around?"

"Koba trusts him and demands proof of what people say Beria is doing."

Beria awoke to hostility and jerked his gaze away from Nadya. His stare wandered over to Eliena Krylenko, where he undressed her with his eyes.

Our reverie was interrupted by Mrs. Voroshilov's call to dinner.

The meal began cordially enough: introductions, smiles, clink of glasses and tinkle of utensils, toasts, and vows of eternal commitment to Socialism amid courses of exquisite foods unimaginable to the masses outside who survived, if at all, on bread and fat drippings.

There were dinners, however, in which the food was delectable, the wine exquisite, the company charming, but these were scarcely noticed because of the charisma of one or two people. When Max Eastman walked into a room, people who did not see or hear him enter turned around. He emanated a presence, a star quality. Seated with him at the same table was Joseph Stalin, a Russian equivalent of great stature. The rest of us faded into irrelevance, nibbling and sipping, as the two giants held sway.

Nadya went over and sat with enormous pride next to her Koba, "the greatest man of the age."

When the clinking of glasses and tableware died down, Stalin spoke, "Comrade Eastman, let me explain what we are undertaking here in the new Soviet Union."

"Please do," Max said, all eyes, ears, and intelligence.

"We will begin to construct Socialism in one country by turning all power over to the people through the Communist Party."

"Will the party in power be elected by the people?" Max asked.

"Of course not," Stalin answered, vaguely annoyed. "The will of the people is expressed by the will of the party." He refilled a tumbler halfway with vodka and tossed it down, neat.

"How does the party determine the will of the people?" Max asked, with quiet reservation.

Stalin stiffened. "The party decides for the people what is right for them, and they accept it."

"What you are describing sounds like a dictatorship," Max said with skepticism.

"Yes. The dictatorship of the proletariat," Stalin said, with an edge.

Nadya began to look ill at ease, and the other guests stared down at their plates.

Max looked up with a wry smile and sober eyes to ask, "What does the party have in mind that is right to do for the people?"

"We will begin by appropriating all means of production in agriculture so that all of the people will share equally in the available food." Stalin poured up two swallows of vodka and drank it.

"Appropriate?" Max asked uneasily.

"We must assemble small farms into large collective farms," Stalin said firmly.

"What about the *kulaks* and *muzhiks*, the small farmers for whom owning land is life itself?"

"We will teach them that collective agriculture is for their own good," Stalin insisted.

"What about their tools and livestock?"

"Combined for the benefit of everyone," Stalin insisted, slurring his words a little.

Max paused reflectively, then leaned forward to ask, "Suppose the farmers are not willing to give up their land, crops, tools, and livestock—without compensation—in exchange for a promise?"

Stalin smiled a tough smile. "We will do our best to persuade them that collective farming will be in their own best interests." He poured another glass of vodka and sipped it.

"Suppose the unthinkable happens, and they put up a fight—breaking tools, hiding crops, and slaughtering livestock?" Max had a skewering look in his eyes.

Stalin's gaze hardened. "We will undertake a massive propaganda and persuasion campaign to persuade the *kulaks* and *muzhiks* that collectivized agriculture is historically inevitable and will lead to happiness for all. They will no longer be a slave to the seasons and the harvests, but they can draw on collective granaries and collective herds for food to feed their families. After all, Comrade Eastman, these are our own people, flesh of our flesh and blood of our blood, and we know they will find happiness through Socialism."

Nadya looked at Stalin with radiant eyes as all the guests rumbled approval.

Max Eastman leaned forward over the table to look Joseph Stalin squarely in the eyes. "I understand your good intentions," he said. "But what will you do if persuasion and good intentions fail? What will you do if they destroy their property rather than turn it over to state control?"

Nadya seemed startled by the prospect.

Stalin said, reluctantly, "Then we would have to regard them as criminals."

"What would you do?" Max persisted.

"I guess…we would have no alternative but to take everything by force."

"Suppose they—physically—put up a fight?"

"Then we would have no choice but to put them into *gulags* or, perhaps, even kill them."

Nadya's mouth dropped open for a moment. She looked at Max and fluttered her hands to make the words go away. "Comrade Eastman, Koba doesn't mean it. His words are only spoken in the heat of debate. It is the vodka that talked about killing."

Stalin turned to her and said through clenched teeth, "Stay out of this—woman!"

Nadya shrank back in her chair and sat wide-eyed.

Stalin looked intently at Max Eastman. "Let there be no mistake about this. Socialism will be created in the Soviet Union by whatever means necessary. By persuasion, if at all possible. By force, if required. It would not matter if eighty percent of them were against Socialism. We would create Socialism if we had to build it on the bones and bodies of the people who oppose us!" He took another swallow of vodka and slammed the glass down.

Nadya clapped the fingers of both hands over her mouth.

Eastman sat thoughtfully for a moment, then asked, "What about industrial development and industrial workers?"

"The factories would have to be confiscated."

"*Gulags* or force?"

"Of course," Stalin said, "but not arbitrarily. Everyone will first be given an opportunity to cooperate."

Max said, "I have seen some of your factories, and they seem pretty backward and inefficient. Do you think the capitalists of the West will offer new technology to modernize them?"

"As Lenin said, the capitalists will sell us the rope to hang them with." Stalin was smug.

"What will you use to buy it? The ruble is almost worthless," Max said skeptically.

Stalin announced, "We will sell agricultural surpluses abroad for hard currency and use the proceeds to buy modem machinery."

"What agricultural surpluses?" Max asked. "Food is scarce. People are hungry."

"Well, then," Stalin snapped, "we will sell whatever is harvested."

"And let the peasants eat grass and twigs?"

"We must industrialize at all costs or be destroyed by the capitalists!"

Max said, skeptically, "That sounds like a recipe for famine."

"Then so be it!" Stalin barked.

Nadya looked horrified by his words.

Eastman's eyes grew tougher. "And what wonderful things will you offer the workers in the factories?"

"Production goals and five-year plans," Stalin rumbled.

"How will you achieve them?"

"Incentives to produce and punishments for not producing."

"Will the workers have a choice of what they will do?" Max inquired.

"Of course not. Every worker will be sent to where he is needed and required to meet a quota."

"What if the new machinery does not come in and the workers cannot meet their goals?"

Stalin's face was beginning to flush with anger. "We will make our own machinery, and workers will meet their production goals."

"Or else?" Max asked.

"Or else!" Stalin responded.

After a long, long moment of silence in which the guests scarcely dared to breathe, Max said flatly, "Your version of Socialism could not be imposed in America. The people would not stand for it. They would fight back ferociously."

Stalin said with finality, "The Russian people will, if imposed with enough force."

Dead silence.

Stalin realized that the party had turned ugly. He leavened the tension by putting tobacco into his pipe, tamping it down, and lighting it. Then he thoughtfully puffed clouds of fragrant smoke. He smiled through a flume and asked, "Why do we look at Socialism so differently?"

Max smiled back, eager for a truce. "I suppose because I am an American and a son of Thomas Jefferson."

"And I," replied Stalin, "am Russian and a son of Ivan the Terrible."

A round of nervous laughter rippled around the dinner table.

Stalin leaned forward, pipe in mouth, to smile at Max Eastman. "The way you think reminds me of John Reed."

Max chuckled. "Jack was a bit of a jerk, personally, but an excellent observer and journalist. That's why I sent him over here to report on the progress of the revolution. As you know, he wrote *Ten Days That Shook the World.*"

"A masterpiece," Stalin said.

Max became sober. "He sent me a later article that was highly critical of what was going on here, then he died."

"Cholera," Stalin said sadly.

"I have talked to people who were with John the night before he died, and they said there was no sign of cholera. One day he was healthy. The next day he was dead and cremated."

"Cholera," Stalin insisted as his eyes went cold. 'Cremated immediately so he could not infect others with cholera. Buried within the walls of the Kremlin with the honors befitting a noble comrade in Socialism and a hero of the Soviet Union."

"How nice," Max said.

Stalin said cuttingly, "Would you like to have him disinterred so you can see the remains?"

"I am allergic to ashes," Max replied.

Stalin smiled reassuringly. "Well, then we have an expression in Russian—*nichevo*—which means, if you cannot do anything about it, relax and think about something else. Shall we put the unfortunate death of John Reed behind us?"

"For now," Max said.

Nadya looked down the table at me with alarmed eyes. As everyone rose from the table, smiling and trying to resurrect conviviality, she left Stalin without a word and wended her way through the crowd to me.

"Philip," she said. "You must not take what Joseph Vissarionovich said seriously. All that talk about force and killing was just that—talk. Koba carried guns to get money for the revolution in the early days, but he has never hurt or killed anyone in his entire life. I know that for a fact. What you just heard was his reaction to the challenges posed by Max Eastman, not anything he would do to his own people. It was rhetoric. Trust me—Joseph Stalin will become the Abraham Lincoln of the Soviet Union and be loved through all time."

Nadya's passion and glowing eyes made me want to believe her ringing words. Then she smiled and turned away to join her husband, who was talking to Max and Eliena.

As she slipped away, I felt a surge of pity. In my research on Stalin, I had learned enough to realize that he was not a womanizer. He was committed to Socialism and had neither the time nor the inclination to play around with other women on the side. His only vice was a pipeful of good tobacco.

Stalin's love poems, filled with yearning and passion, were obviously written for his first wife, his *grand amour,* Ekaterina Svanidze. The slight yellowing of the paper hinted at their age. Nadya had created the myth of the "other woman" to explain the existence of the poems and to smother her visceral jealousy of Ekaterina. Nadya had at least a chance to compete with a flesh-and-blood woman, but she could not compete with a ghost, a memory. It was a harmless self-delusion. As I looked at lovely Nadya across the crowded room, I decided to go along with her self-delusion and pretend to look for the "other woman." After all, a woman who loves can talk herself into believing anything.

Nadya deserved a poem. I decided to write one for her, during some interstice of time, and present it to her on an appropriate occasion. She needed a poem to ease the pain of knowing that she inspired no poetry in her husband.

In the meanwhile, I remembered that I had a job to do, and I drifted through the crowd to make a closer acquaintance with Max Eastman. He was a brilliant intellectual who had a way of cutting through bullshit to get to the truth of things. I liked him. Perhaps he could even add some tidbits to history.

I joined them at the edges just in time to enjoy Stalin's wit and pointed sense of humor.

Max said, "What will you do if there is a Communist revolution in Germany?"

"There will not be a peoples' revolution in Germany because the Germans are like sheep. Where the ram goes, the others follow. Besides, there would never be a revolution in Germany because somebody might have to step on the lawns."

Max and I laughed at this lively thrust and enjoyed what followed. Stalin had a restless temperament. He questioned himself and others and argued with himself and others. Despite his passionate and many-sided nature, however, I sensed he was a cold calculator. He trusted what was within his fist, and anyone or anything beyond his clutch was a potential enemy.

How could I write this in the biography of Joseph Stalin? Nadya would never agree.

15

What do they know
who plow the fields with their backs?
Can they read the future
and see the shining joy of generations to come?

—Joseph Stalin

"I had never seen Joseph Stalin so wildly enthusiastic," I grumbled as a jolt awakened me to stare at the dark ceiling of the railroad car. "It was the first brick laid in the road to hell."

"Look at these harvest production figures!" Stalin exulted. This sober, steady man was beside himself with excitement.

Max and Eliena, Nadya and I—now a regular foursome—huddled around Stalin's huge desk, a smear of graphs, charts, reports, and documents covering the surface. The walls of Koba's office in the Kremlin, once decorated with pictures of Marx, Engels, and Lenin, were now festooned with maps of agricultural areas—especially Ukraine.

Stalin picked up a summary page and dangled it before Max's eyes. "I told you that persuasion would do it—the farms are being collectivized, and production of grain has gone up over twenty percent." He was euphoric with success, the happiest I had ever seen him.

Max Eastman walked around looking intently at maps, reports, plans, and then back to the maps, visibly impressed by the documents of change.

Nadya beamed at her husband with enormous pride and glanced an I-told-you-so smile at me.

I too was impressed. I had held my breath when Stalin seized the reins of power—squeezing out Zinoviev and Kamenev—but his timing was perfect as always. Now he was forging ahead with his agenda for Socialism in one country, and so far, so good.

Max said seriously, "All this looks like good material for an article in *New Masses* magazine."

Stalin grinned like a teenager. "There are no fortresses that cannot by conquered by Communism." His Asiatic eyes glowed and crackled as he rattled off predictions of 30 percent, 50 percent, 100 percent in two to five years. He was possessed by the idea that by the single stroke of setting production goals to be met by the farmers, he could bring about the transformation of Russia.

I watched fascinated. He seemed to be existing in a half-real and half-dream world of industrial orders and instructions, statistical figures, and indices. Stalin was almost wild-eyed with this early success, a fantasy world in which no target and no objectives seemed unrealistic. He was talking almost to himself as he ranted on about the future of the Soviet Union. As I listened to his economic projections, I said to myself, *chistaya fantasiya*, "pure fantasy."

Stalin paused, about to boast. "When Peter the Great began to build factories and workshops to supply his armies to face the West, he had to deal with the backwardness of the social order. The new structure of Soviet society—where orders are given and obeyed—creates incomparably better conditions for development. By setting production goals and enforcing them, the Soviet Union will achieve glory that Peter the Great could only dream about!"

This was my first insight that Joseph Stalin is fanatical and, perhaps, ruthless.

Max paused in his perusal of maps. He looked up quizzically and said, "I spent yesterday in the farmer's market and had the impression that there was much less food for sale than before."

Stalin smiled and shrugged reassuringly. "That could be for any of several reasons. A lull between crops. Transportation problems. Whatever."

Max nodded and said, "What about industrial production?"

"Also up over twenty percent. Max and Stalin walked over to a stack of reports and conferred privately, their backs turned toward us.

Nadya turned to me to speak confidentially. "You are seeing the real Joseph Vissarionovich at work for the party and the people. Planning the organization of work, of farming, of industry. Assigning responsibilities and seeing to it they are carried out. Lenin himself recognized the organizational genius of Joseph Stalin, and now you see that confidence fulfilled."

I nodded in the face of feminine pride.

"You see," she murmured firmly, waving her hand at the whirlwind of documented activities, "Koba is abreast of everything. He is so brilliant that he remembers every detail, organizes it in context, and acts on it for the benefit of the people."

My instinct was to mock her a little, but as I looked about, I felt a sense of greatness here. What I could not tell Nadya was that her enchanting presence overwhelmed all other persons and activities. She obliterated my awareness of almost everything except Nadya. Manfully, I struggled to return to my job—looking, listening, remembering so that I could add more pages to the sheaves of scribbled paper in a box that would become the biography of Joseph Stalin. And I wondered how what I had written would be received. Try as I might, the words honestly recorded what I saw, heard, and felt, and my perceptions of Joseph Stalin were all too human. Darling Nadya wanted a written version of a white marble equestrian statue, but the best I could manage was a biography that revealed him as a man, warts and all. That is, the warts he would allow me to see. He had not so far granted me a private interview.

Max and Stalin turned back toward us, smiling and talking anxiously, seemingly *po dusham*, "heart-to-heart."

Stalin was in a persuasion mode with Max. "Remember that we are tearing a wooden plow from the hands of a hundred million peasants and placing those hands on the wheels of the tractor. Remember that we are forcing millions of people into schools and making them learn how to read and write. All this is for the ultimate good of the people, whether they like it or not The party knows best."

Max smiled with reserve. "I think that what you say is probably true, but you must understand that I must go to those collective farms and see the facts for myself."

"But why? These reports are all *pravda*—truth. Why not just use the reports to further the cause of Socialism in your article?" Stalin was baffled.

Max explained, "The ground rules of American journalism require that I see the facts for myself before I publish it as true. If I write or publish anything in *New Masses* that is not true, the magazine will lose its credibility. And the capitalist press will have a party with it."

Stalin paused, listening, and then said, "Our system is better. We tell the Russian people only what is good for them to know so they will cooperate with the party—which in turn acts on their behalf."

Max smiled gently, a bit tired of the ideological struggle. "That may be so in Russia, but in America, I must confirm the facts for myself before I can publish them."

Stalin frowned, but nodded and said, "Do what you have to do." He turned to Nadya and spoke as a commissar. "Comrade Alliluyeva is assigned to facilitate everything that Comrade Eastman needs to see to write his article for *New Masses* magazine." He nodded at me and added, "I want Comrade Makharov to join them to gather notes for the biography.

I was surprised to be invited along, surprised that he gave a thought to his biography. Great things were in the offing, and he wanted posterity to appreciate him. I admitted to myself that Koba was being as *po dusham* in his openness as anyone could ask for. His credibility was high.

Lavrentiy Beria appeared in the room. None of us saw him enter, but there he was. There was something lacquered looking about him.

Stalin said, "Lavrentiy, I am busy. Whatever it is, can't it wait?"

"No," Beria replied and solemnly handed him a report, which Stalin took and began to read. Beria flicked his gaze over to Eliena, whose beauty looked like a voluptuous flower, and over to Nadya, whose unflinching stare made him look away.

"I don't believe this!" Stalin exclaimed and looked around. "*Kulaks* are withholding crops to force higher prices! Some are refusing to join collective farms!"

"That sounds familiar," Max commented.

Stalin clenched his fist. "The *kulaks* will not be allowed to do this to Socialism—or to *me!* We can increase food production by fifty percent a year through collective farming. We can sell the surpluses for hard currency to buy machinery to industrialize! We must do this. We must!" In a rage, he turned on Beria and grabbed him by the coat lapels to smash him back against the wall, where he slammed him again and again.

We were appalled by the explosion of violence.

Nadya leaped forward to pull Stalin away and shouted, "Koba! Koba! What are you doing?"

Beria stammered, "I only brought the message…"

Stalin swept back his arm, and Nadya was staggered to the desk.

We stood stunned to see the rage in Stalin's face. This sober, solid man had lost all self-control.

Nadya stared at her husband, her eyes wide and her lips parted.

Max Eastman saved the awful moment by stepping forward and saying, "When we see what is going on out there, we will bring the facts to you."

Stalin stopped and regained his poise. He smiled his appreciation at being saved from himself. He said to Max, "Thank you, comrade." He walked over to the map of Ukraine and ran his palm over it. "It is absolutely vital that we proceed with collectivized agriculture because everything else depends on getting hard currency for grain sales. If the *kulaks* try to play capitalist games with us, we will launch an all-out offensive against them and smash them—eliminate them as a class. We will strike at the *kulaks* so hard as to prevent them from ever rising to their feet again. We will break down their resistance in open battle with no quarter given or asked." Stalin strode back to his desk with his rage rising again and smashed his fist on a stack of reports. "We will build Socialism in Russia and crush anyone who stands in our way."

Nadya tore her gaze from him to look at me, her face white with shock. Was this her Koba?

Then Stalin placed his palms flat on the reports of success and murmured, "Peter the Great."

Nadya heard his words and stared at her husband as if she were seeing Joseph Stalin for the first time.

I wondered what place all this should have in his biography.

16

Why is it that wherever I go
the flowers die,
the leaves wither,
and the earth loses its fragrance?

—Joseph Stalin

"Ukraine," I murmured, shuddering at what it had done to Nadya. The train rumbled and jerked to a halt with metallic clanging noises as each railroad car was slowed by impact with the preceding car. I awakened to pitch darkness. The guards, Hog and Squeaky, sounded as if they were sitting up. After a long hissing moment, however, the locomotive began to chug heavily, and the train again lumbered into action. Hog and Squeaky muttered obscenities, then lay down again and were enveloped in blankets and darkness. In my exhaustion, the warmth of blankets and the cradle-rocking motion soon lulled me back into memory.

Madness first crept into Nadya's eyes during our boat trip to Ukraine, a journey too dangerous in these times to undertake on a train or in automobiles. She used her clout to requisition and provision a river yacht (the treasure of an oil magnate since stood up against a wall), with sleeping cabins, galley, and crew, to sail down the Dnieper River through Ukraine—the bread basket of the Soviet Union and scene of the first attempt at collective farming.

As Stalin had suggested, Nadya had brought along Max and Eliena for the article in *New Masses* and me, so I could write about this glorious episode for his biography. We set off in a festive spirit of adventure as if going on an extended holiday to celebrate the successes of collective farming. We enjoyed the pleasures of standing at the railing, wind in our hair and sun in our faces and blue skies above, to look out at a flat horizon that seemed to extend to forever.

The first nasty shock came when Nadya spied Red Guards setting up machine guns around the hovel and barn of a family of *kulaks*. A man was urging three goats and a cow into the barn. Nadya ordered the yacht pulled over to the bank. Front and rear anchors were dropped and a gangplank lowered to the grassy bank. She led the way as we stomped down and walked through the grass to the commanding officer.

"What on earth are you doing?" Nadya demanded.

The grizzled and fiftyish officer stared owlishly at her party card, held under his nose, identifying her as Stalin's wife. He stammered, "I am setting up machine guns."

"I can see that for myself!" Nadya shouted. "The question is why?"

"The peasants have refused to surrender their grain and livestock to the state and refuse to move to a collective farm." The officer had the face of a battered barn door.

Nadya stared at him incredulously. "Are you actually going to carry out the slaughter of a family of innocent people in order to confiscate their grain and livestock?"

"I am obeying orders," he said. He bowed his head and looked miserable.

"Whose orders?" Nadya barked.

"Comrade Stalin has issued a general order to seize the grain and animals of the kulaks and to execute all who do not obey."

Nadya gasped. "Koba? That cannot be!" She stood for a long, stunned moment as the implications sank in. Then she clenched her fists and strode over to stand before one of the machine guns aimed at the family of terrified peasants. She announced, "Before you kill them, you must kill Stalin's wife." She crossed her arms.

The officer bowed his head again and said, "Thank you for stopping me." He looked at her, opened hamlike hands, and reached toward her, hands caked with dirt and fingers like gnarled sausages. "How could it come to this? I fought for Mother Russia in the Great

War and was wounded many times. I fought in the Red Army in countless bloody battles in the civil war and survived as my comrades died around me. My family was murdered on their farm by the whites while I was away fighting them on another front. Did I live through all that horror to end by giving an order to fire on my own people? Am I to do to others what was done to my own family?" His reddened eyes blinked back tears, and he murmured, "No, no, no."

Nadya stood there listening and softening. Then she pointed her finger at the machine gunner before her. "Stalin's wife orders you to take that thing down."

The machine gunner, himself a peasant grown gray in the wars, smiled with relief. He glanced up at the officer, who nodded, and he lifted the gun from its tripod. Two other machine gunners dismantled their machine guns.

Max Eastman, who had stood in silent witness, said, "So that explains the increase in grain production for the state. They are stealing it at gunpoint." He wrote thoughtfully on a notepad. Max glanced at the peasant family now standing before the house, looking enormously relieved. He said, "I think I'll talk to them." Eliena took his arm and walked step for step with him through the stubble to the house.

Nadya walked over to stand beside me and turned to stare at Max and Eliena talking and gesturing to the family. She said, "I cannot believe that Koba would give such an order."

"Goodbye, comrades," a voice said, and we glanced up to see the Red Guard commander leading his detachment away with machine guns on their shoulders.

Nadya called out, "Give me that general order."

The commander took it out of a chest pocket and gave it to her, saluted, and rejoined his men.

Nadya opened the folded paper and read it. "Koba will need to explain this," she said.

We stood reflectively and watched Max and Eliena conferring with the family and Max taking notes. Eventually, we could see Max wrap it up by closing his notebook and shaking hands with the men. Eliena did her thing by showering hugs and kisses on men, women, and children alike. They waved goodbye to the grinning peasants and marched back to us.

Max said, "They have been ordered to deliver more grain than they have harvested, and they are not being allowed to keep their seed corn."

"In exchange for what?" Nadya asked.

"In exchange for a piece of paper promising a tractor when it is eventually produced."

"But that would leave them with nothing to eat!" Nadya protested. "Nothing to plant for a new crop!"

"Nothing at all," Max said matter-of-factly, with a cold look in his blue eyes.

Nadya announced, in denial, "Koba could not possibly have known of the real consequences of this order. He could not intend that people should die. I cannot believe it!"

I spoke out for the first time. "The general order of confiscation was signed by Joseph Stalin, who stipulated the execution of those who did not comply. You just read the order."

We three stood and stared at one another, not knowing what to say, not wanting to hurt Nadya.

The silence was broken by the approach of two of the peasant women from the house, each leading a small child. Neither of the women was much over thirty, but each looked at least fifty. Their figures were shapeless from a diet of bread and jam; they were stooped from labor in the fields. Their hands were thickened and dirty, their heads were covered with *babushkas*, and they wore the plainest of patched gray dresses. Yet they walked with the measured stateliness of icons emerging from the soul of Ukraine.

Then they stood before us. A little girl of six or so ducked behind her mother's skirts and peered shyly out from behind her mother. The other woman had a boy about eight years old who doubled his grip on his mother's hand and stared bravely at us. The tension was palpable, but nothing snapped social strain like the charm of children.

Nadya's face radiated maternal warmth as she sank to her heels and extended a coaxing arm to each child. She smiled and asked in a lilting voice, "What are your names?"

Both mothers smiled back and encouraged their children to step forward and introduce themselves. They did so, timorously, with many looks back.

Nadya took the hand of the dirty but pretty tousle-headed little girl, who stared uneasily at her with huge blue eyes. She asked again, "What is your name?"

The girl mumbled, "Sonja."

"How lovely!" Nadya exclaimed. "And yours?"

The boy grimaced and said, "Sergei."

"Sonja and Sergei! How perfect!"

Sonja's mother waited a moment, then asked, diffidently, "May we speak to Stalin's wife?"

Nadya stood up and assumed her role, while Sonja and Sergei scampered behind their mothers.

The woman was worried, but she steeled herself. She said, "We farm people have a way of life we have lived for a long time. It is a hard but a happy life. We raise enough food to feed our families and, in good years, enough surplus to sell for rubles to buy what we cannot make. Would you be so kind as to tell your husband, Comrade Stalin, that this way of life suits us? We wish to pass the land and the life on to our children and grandchildren. We do not wish to exchange it for a collective farm in which we have nothing of our own, no lives of our own, and what we produce will be taken away from us by the state."

Nadya said, "Try to understand that wise people in the government are making plans to give your families a much better life and a better future."

The woman looked concerned. "We believe that the leaders of the revolution are all city people who think like city people. They are book people who cannot plan for farmers because they do not understand farming. They believe in things that exist only in words. They look at the world through books, and the words keep them from seeing life as it is. They talk themselves into believing ideas that are crazy to us and then force their will upon those who live on the land. They do not want to understand us and want only that we should do what they say, no matter how hurtful or hateful to us. To them, books are gods. People are nothing." She clapped her hand to her mouth, appalled by what she had said and afraid of consequences.

A chord was struck in Nadya. She stepped forward to touch the woman's arm reassuringly and said, "I will tell Comrade Stalin." Nadya turned to include the other woman and asked, "How long have you lived on this land?"

"Always. We are sisters, and our families have lived and died here forever."

Nadya said, "Thank you for speaking your hearts to me."

The sisters beamed at each other, curtsied to Nadya, then walked back to the house and the waiting men. Their children tore loose from their mother's hands and ran yelling to their fathers, who scooped them up into their arms.

We four—Nadya, Max, Eliena, and I—were no longer individual people seeing things in an individual way but bonded together as a distraught bundle of humanity.

Nadya said, "We must see all that is happening on the farms. We must know everything before I confront my husband."

Dinner that evening began in near silence, broken only by a slight rocking of the yacht and the lapping of the river against the sides. Each of us was lost in sober thoughts after seeing machine guns being set up to slaughter a farm family. We were unsettled and apprehensive.

"Those children," Nadya said uneasily, "could be my children. Sergei and Sonja could be Vassily and Svetlana."

We had no answer for that. The face of impending tragedy binds people together. We sat around the small table, feeling an invisible bond that brought us together as one.

The steward brought bowls of excellent *borscht*, but Nadya sat and stared at her food.

"Please eat," I urged.

Nadya put a spoonful into her mouth and tasted it thoughtfully. Then spoon in hand, she again stared at her plate. Sometimes, she glanced about at us with dark, anxious eyes but again returned to gaze down at her food. We were on eggshells not to upset her.

Max leaned forward with kind blue eyes to say, "We have only seen what did not happen. Perhaps the order to kill will not be carried out. It may be that there has been a change of heart, and the order has been withdrawn. So as far as we know, there has been no harm done."

Eliena suddenly flowered a smile and chimed in, "So far, there has been no harm done."

I who loved Nadya said nothing because I could see she was almost inward, beyond our reach.

Nadya brightened a little at the hopeful thoughts, then arose quietly, murmuring, "Excuse me," and turned to climb up the stairs with quiet steps and out onto the deck. Her meal was cold and almost untouched.

I glanced at Max and Eliena for tacit approval to leave. They nodded, and I stood up to follow Nadya up into the evening.

Sunset had passed. An indigo blanket of dark sky was settling down as stars appeared to begin their evening twinkles. A soft breeze brought the scents of the earth and plants and flowing water to my nostrils, and it was like the breath of heaven.

I turned about and saw Nadya leaning against the railing near the bow of the boat, staring at a piece of paper in her hand. She glanced up at the sound of my approaching footsteps, but there was no smile of greeting. Nadya looked away at the darkening river and shivered a little at the first chill of approaching night.

I stood quietly beside her and asked—"May I?"—and put my arm about her shoulders.

She nodded and snuggled a little toward the warmth of me.

"A lovely evening," I said.

"I hadn't noticed."

"Try to enjoy it," I added, but she said nothing.

After a long moment, Nadya held up the general order and whispered, "I cannot believe that my Koba issued this death sentence for the innocent." Then she shouted, "My Koba did this!" She shook her head and turned away to hide her feelings.

I leaned before her, savoring the intimacy of the moment and the warmth of her body under my arm. I said, gently, "Perhaps it was written by Beria, and he slipped it into a stack of documents to sign. Your Koba may have been so busy with other matters that he scribbled his name on the general order without actually reading it. Such things happen."

"Philip," she said firmly, looking at me. "This is a license to kill. Any family that refuses to surrender its grain, livestock, tools—everything they have—will be slaughtered. Any family that agrees to surrender them will starve. It means death if they do and death if they don't. Even Lavrentiy Beria would not dare to trick Joseph Stalin into signing such a document. This is an order of such horrific possible consequences that it would only have been issued by the head of the Communist Party—my husband! This is monstrous!"

"It may be just a bluff to make peasants surrender most of their grain, but not all of it."

Nadya turned to me abruptly, and I withdrew my arm. She waved the order and shouted, "Those Red Guards would have murdered that peasant family if we had not happened along! This order has gone out all over Ukraine, and I tremble to think of what we will find!"

I was crushed into silence by her outburst.

She suddenly stopped, breathing heavily, drained by her explosion of emotion. Then she murmured, "Thank you, Philip, for trying to console me, for trying to make excuses for my husband. You have a good heart… And now, if you don't mind, I would prefer to be alone."

I felt rejected but kissed her on the forehead, Russian style, and she smiled around the corners of her mouth.

I turned and walked the length of the deck to the stairwell, then glanced back. Nadya was still staring down at the order to kill, and I sensed through the lowering darkness that she was swallowed up by gloom and dread.

A glance upward before going below revealed a sky now clouding over, but the fragrance of earth and water followed me down into the bowels of the yacht.

The next morning, the yacht weighed anchor, and as the vessel got underway, we stood at the railing to enjoy Ukraine's vast expanse of yellow and blue. We felt joy in the morning, but the land was now stripped as far as the eye could see. And where were the birds?

We saw a peasant woman peer out of a mud-and-thatch hovel, then come running toward us, waving her arms, followed by three emaciated children, all girls.

"Pull over to the bank," Nadya ordered. The yacht turned and scraped along the embankment, and a crewman dropped a holding anchor.

"We are hungry!" the hungry woman shouted from within her *babushka*. "Please! At least feed my children!"

The gangplank went down, and we trooped down to meet the scarecrow woman and her brood. Starvation was etched on their faces.

Nadya asked, "Where is your man?"

"Shot and killed," the woman groaned, waving arms that looked like sticks. "He fought to stop the Red Guards from taking our grain, and they filled him full of bullets." She pointed to a mound of dirt, near the hutch, with two sticks tied together as a cross. "He is buried there." Then she turned to Nadya and begged, *"Slava Bogu.* We are starving."

"What have you been living on?"

"Weeds and water."

"Wait here," Nadya said and nodded for Eliena to follow her up to the yacht.

Within ten minutes, they were tottering down the gangplank with a kettle of hot cabbage soup, spoons, and a loaf of black bread.

Max and I hurried over to take the kettle from them and carry it to the hungry family. We placed the steaming soup on the ground. The woman and her three children surrounded it, snatched spoons, tore off chunks of bread, and began to eat ravenously.

We four stood and watched them devour their feed, shaken by their desperation. The children were skinny ragamuffins, dressed in rags, but sweet and gentle creatures like their mother. One girl was so weak she had trouble feeding herself, but the other two helped her.

When at last they were full, there was a third of a kettle of soup left and two heels of bread.

"May we keep this for another meal?" the woman begged.

Nadya nodded, her dark eyes moist, then turned to me and asked, "Philip, would you please go to the galley and bring four loaves of bread for them."

"Where are they kept?"

Eliena insisted, "I'll get them. I know where they are stored." She scampered up to the yacht to return with four round loaves of black bread.

The peasant woman smelled them when Eliena handed them over and smiled gratefully. She gave a loaf to each of her children to hold. They stood and watched solemnly as we returned to the yacht, and the crew cast off.

"*Spasibo!*" the woman called out in thanks.

Migod, I thought, looking at the pitiful family. *This is only the beginning.*

Nadya stared stone-faced at the mother and children until they disappeared around a bend in the river. Then her gaze lowered, and she stared down at the wake behind the yacht to await the next evidence of the general order.

As we cruised down the Dnieper River, apparitions seemed to emerge from the earth to wail piteously for food, so many that we did not dare to go ashore for fear of being mobbed. Mothers held up or pointed to their hungry children. Old people opened their gap-toothed mouths and rubbed their stomachs. Dangerous-looking men stood in sullen clusters to watch us pass, sometimes shaking clenched fists. The crowds grew in numbers into desperate groups who walked along the banks to glower threateningly at us, as if we were capitalist tourists coming to enjoy their misery and suffering. We sensed that some of them were looking for a chance to get at us and take what we had. Now we became wary and concerned for our own safety.

Periodically, the yacht began to bump into corpses floating in the river, probably those that had drowned themselves. The bodies of those who had extended their lives by living on weeds and water until death came could be seen shining in cadaverous whiteness along the shallow embankments. The scent of putrid decay was becoming awful.

That evening, we anchored in the center of the river in fear of being attacked. There were small islands in the river, but we were afraid a group might swim out to them, so we decided to stay the night in the center of the stream. When we went out on deck to take the evening air after a guilty dinner of ham and potatoes, we instead inhaled the sweet, sickly smell of death. The stench of rotting bodies hung in the air like a miasmic fog of sewage, accompanied by hordes of flies and mosquitoes that soon drove us down below. We slammed shut all the doors and portholes to close out the horrors of dying Ukraine.

We sat in a circle around our little table, looking morosely at a candle flickering in the center, listening to distant calls, wails, and curses from the embankment.

We were all in shock, but Nadya was shaken to the marrow of her soul. Her eyes opened so wide that we could see the whites all around. She talked in mumbles as if we were not there. We did our best not to be there but sat in silences that scarcely dared to exchange a look.

Nadya withdrew into herself and simply did not see us. She lived inside her own world and related only to what she found there.

I died inside watching her.

None of us could think of a thing to say or do for her.

Nadya stared vacantly into space as if from an unoccupied body. Her eyes rimmed with tears, and she groaned, "How could you? How *could* you?" Then she emotionally rejoined us and said quietly, "We must see everything."

Max said bluntly, "Everything we see will be described fully in *New Masses* magazine. I will not hold back anything in deference to the cause of Socialism, in deference to your feelings or the feelings of Joseph Stalin."

Nadya took my arm and said, "I would not have it any other way. Nor would I have Philip lie in his biography of Koba."

Then the horrors of famine began and deepened as we cruised down the river, day by day, week by week. The countryside soon looked as if a swarm of locusts had eaten everything to the ground. We saw one field that seemed to be pulsating on the surface; when we went ashore to investigate, we found thousands of starving mice scurrying through the stubble, trying to find something to eat. Emaciated people, looking like skeletons, wailed and begged for food. We began to find human bodies everywhere: in ravines, in fields, floating in the river, in abandoned houses, sitting dead against the sides of hovels. Everywhere, there was the sickly stench of death.

Whenever a child was found alive, Nadya prepared some of our food to feed the youngster.

We stopped to investigate a farmhouse that should have had people in it and found a family of four hanging by their necks, dead, with a note saying, "We cannot live any longer in this hell."

Nadya, in the face of unspeakable tragedy, was talking to herself and listening to voices that she answered out loud. Max, Eliena, and I saw what was happening to her, and we stayed close and were attentive to her. But with the discovery of yet another dead body, emaciated person, or starving child, she would burst into tears and weep uncontrollably.

Whole villages were without life. In the deathly silence, nothing could be heard, neither the barking of dogs nor the mewing of cats, nor the chirping of birds or the croaking of ravens since all these creatures had long since been eaten. Some of the houses stood with open doors or shutters, while in others, they had been removed to fire the stoves, and there were only black spaces showing. Bodies were lying about in the weeds and in the houses, and an incredibly putrid smell filled the air. Occasionally, there were mothers who still had the strength to move who grubbed for roots or gathered the seeds of weeds so they could, at least, boil these for their starving children

Ukraine was a wasteland.

And Nadya's eyes acquired a strange expression that never left her. She seemed to be not quite present even when we talked to her.

We saw Red Guards arresting people who were only gleaning in fields for the grains that had fallen. In wheat fields as yet not harvested, we saw armed men, some in towers, ready to kill the farmers who sought to eat the wheat they had planted, though families sometimes crept in at night to chew nourishment from the wheat heads. When caught, they were shot.

Then we arrived at Kiev, where the food stores were closed and the churches were open. Starving people had limped and crawled into the city to find work and food, but not finding either, they filled the churches to beg help from the Almighty. The streets groaned with body wagons filled with corpses collected from under bridges, from gutters and ditches, and from anywhere they had dropped in their tracks. Bodies were heaved into the wagons as if they were bags of garbage.

We became increasingly alarmed by the maniacal look in Nadya's eyes.

Nadya kept saying, "I must see more! I must see more!"

"Nadya!" I urged, holding her tightly with an arm around her shoulders. "We dare not go on to Poltava and Dnieperstroy, or it will drive us all mad. I hear that it is even worse there. Besides, you have given away so much food that we will starve to death ourselves if we don't return to Moscow. It will only be more of the same—people starving to death by the millions."

Nadya looked at me with flat, dispirited eyes and murmured, "It did not need to happen. Our revolution did this to them. Koba did this to them."

I nodded.

"Let's go home," she said.

We returned to the yacht and began our journey back to Moscow, each lost in our thoughts.

Max spread out his notes on a galley table and wrote his article for *New Masses* magazine as we traveled. I took out my notebook and worked on material for the biography of Joseph Stalin, material I knew had to be written but I also knew would never be published.

Nadya sat and stared at nothing. She looked beaten, diminished, disillusioned. There was no more talk of Joseph Stalin being the Abraham Lincoln of the Soviet Union. Her god had failed.

As I sat working on Stalin's biography, I watched her from the corner of my eye. My empathy went out to the woman who had lost her love and her reason for existence. Stalin had broken her heart by his heartlessness, and by never having written poems for her as he had for another woman, he had wounded her inner being. Nadya deserved a poem from a man who loved her. I pulled out a sheet of paper and began to write. I am not a poet, and what I write could not touch the beauty of Stalin's work, but I would now inscribe a poem for Nadya and give it to her at the right emotional time.

When Max finished the first draft of his article, written in English, he read it to us, translated into Russian. It told the story of a man-made famine in Ukraine imposed for political reasons.

Nadya listened, completely wrung out, and murmured, "It's all true. Every word of it is true."

As the boat chugged upriver, we saw the house and barns of the kulak family we had visited earlier, now a scene of ruin and devastation like the rest of Ukraine.

Nadya leaped to her feet and said, "I want to see Sonja and Sergei to bring them food."

The yacht was anchored at the bank, and we strode down the gangplank once more. We walked through the stubble to where we saw the same two women sitting now beside a fire made from the wood of a door. They were gaunt and emaciated but nodded in recognition of Nadya. We looked about at the devastation of the house and barn.

Max asked, "Where are the men? What happened?"

The mother of Sonja looked up and said, "People from the next village had all their grain and livestock taken by the Red Guards. They were left with nothing to eat. They were starving and came here. They killed our men and took all of our grain and livestock and left us with nothing. It was soon after you left."

Nadya asked, hesitantly, "What have you had to eat all this time? Where are Sonja and Sergei? Have they wandered away?"

"Sergei was killed in the attack, and Sonja died later. There was nothing left to eat, and we were starving, so we used them as food. I ate Sergei, and she ate Sonja. It was easier that way." She pointed to a child's hand charred in the ashes.

Nadya stared at the little hand and screamed, "Vassily! Svetlana!"

"No," the woman intoned, vacantly. "Sergei and Sonja."

Nadya turned to me with insane eyes and shouted, "Joseph Stalin will answer for this!" She was cauterized of all illusions and was never the same after Ukraine.

17

> I must play the waiting game,
> and watch for my enemy's weakness.
> Sooner or later is all the same,
> for I will catch him sleeping.
>
> —Joseph Stalin

The train jangled past a hamlet in which I glimpsed four people standing in the snow talking earnestly about something. It triggered the memory of how Max, Eliena, Nadya, and I had met in Gorky Park, on a freezing day, to discuss how to save Max Eastman from the fate of John Reed.

Max said, "My article about famine in Ukraine has been intercepted by Soviet authorities. I have received two cables from the acting editor of *New Masses* asking why I haven't contacted him. The fact is that I have sent several cables, and they have all been stopped. This is exactly what happened when I sent John Reed over to report on the Bolshevik revolution. I sent cable after cable, with no answer, and then I heard he had died."

I could see that Max was grimly worried, squinting his blue eyes in the face of the icy wind.

Eliena was so frightened her hands trembled. "I have made inquiries through my job at the foreign office and found that Stalin has sealed all the borders of the Soviet Union against the departure of anyone named Max Eastman. Max is trapped here. In time, he will be killed!"

Nadya pulled up the fur collar of her greatcoat and turned her back to the driving freezing wind. "We must act as soon as possible. Koba has read a copy of Max's article, and it drove him into a drunken rage. Joseph yelled that he was going to give Max Eastman the same treatment he gave John Reed. I did not think it was possible until we went to Ukraine, but I have come to realize that my Koba, my beloved husband, my heroic revolutionary, is changing into something else—a self-serving killer." Her eyes were wide open, and moisture rimmed.

Eliena whimpered, "We cannot let Max be murdered."

Something occurred to Nadya. She said, "Do you two love each other enough to marry?"

Max grinned widely. "We've talked about it."

Eliena smiled and said, "In a minute."

Nadya said, "In Russia, a marrying couple can take the name of the woman if they choose. If Max and Eliena get married and take her name, he then becomes Max Krylenko. The marriage documents issued to him in that name should enable him to acquire a Soviet passport in the name of Krylenko. Then you will be on your way out of the Soviet Union."

I said, "Trying for a Soviet passport will be a dicey business."

"Not with Stalin's wife standing there and ordering it. They would not dare to refuse me."

"What about his accent?" I asked. "His Russian is good, but he has an accent."

Nadya looked imperiously at me. "The Soviet Union is a polyglot nation that contains a hundred weird languages and dialects. We'll tell them that Max is from Siberia, and they will not question his accent. Stalin's wife will be standing beside them when they marry and then apply for a passport They will do as I say, or else."

Max was concerned. "If this comes to the attention of Stalin, you will be in a heap of trouble with your husband."

"My husband is in trouble with me," Nadya said. "John Reed is buried within the walls of the Kremlin because Joseph Stalin put him there. One murdered American is enough."

Max asked, "Do you know how he died?"

Nadya answered, "It wasn't cholera as they said. Reed was shot and then cremated immediately so there could not be an autopsy."

"How do you know?" I asked.

Nadya smiled wryly. "Nobody knows a man as well as his wife. When he was in a drunken rage over Max's article about famine in the Ukraine, I wheedled the details out of him."

"But why was he killed?" Max asked.

Nadya glanced up at Max. "John Reed wrote an article that warned against the rise of Joseph Stalin. Your article on famine in the Ukraine placed the responsibility for the suffering we saw squarely on Joseph Stalin."

A moment of dead silence allowed the implications to sink in. Max Eastman would be a dead man if they did not take action immediately.

Nadya took charge. "We will go down to the government offices right now to marry Max and Eliena. Philip and I will be witnesses."

Russian government offices were essentially huge, dark, gloomy, and tomb-like, with long lines of people extending into infinity from every clerk at every open service window. A line of young couples with glum, shuttered faces began at the marriage license window and straggled out into the corridor, down the hall, and into the street.

Nadya looked at the line and said, "We don't have two days to wait." She strode to the head of the line and presented her party card.

The clerk had his head down over some documents and snapped, "I'm busy. Wait in line like everybody else."

Nadya thrust her identity card between his eyes and the paperwork, so he was forced to read it.

He looked up, wide-eyed, and gasped, "Stalin's wife!" He clicked his heels and bowed deeply.

The couples near the front of the line, when they heard who she was, squeezed back to make room, as if she were an emissary from the devil.

Nadya turned and snapped her fingers. Max and Eliena came forward with guilty eyes to step in at the head of the line. Max murmured *spasibo*, "thank you," to the next couple.

The clerk looked quizzically at Max but indicated how to fill out and sign the marriage forms.

He asked them, "What is your chosen married name?"

"Krylenko," Max said.

The clerk looked vaguely surprised but said nothing. He stamped the marriage documents with the imprimatur of the state, and the papers were signed and delivered to Max and Eliena. The clerk smiled and said, "Congratulations and best wishes to the Krylenkos."

Nadya asked, "Where do they do the civil ceremonies?"

"Upstairs," the clerk said.

Nadya led the charge up a rickety stairway that was as dark as a catacomb. We trailed after her to find another seemingly endless line of young couples waiting with the dogged queue-line patience unique to the Russian people.

Nadya went to the head of the line and repeated her performance of presenting her identity card, striking terror into the hearts of everyone and hustling Max and Eliena through the civil ceremony ahead of everyone else.

"Witnesses?" a bureaucrat asked. Nadya and I signed our names to the document.

Nadya announced, "You are now legally Max and Eliena Krylenko."

Max grinned. "Without your clout, we'd have been in line for two days."

I smiled at Nadya. "You're shameless."

She looked airily at me and said, "One must have *some* privileges, or what's the point of being at the top of the pile?"

I smiled at her adorable arrogance.

"Now," she said, looking at Max and Eliena, "passports." Nadya marched out of this building and down the street to another government building as dreary as the first. Again, there were long lines from the passport windows, and again Nadya marched to the head of the line and bullied her way in. Max and Eliena made out the appropriate forms, and the clerk said, "The passports will be ready in a month."

"You will process them now," Nadya said with a hard-eyed look.

"Quite impossible," the clerk said.

"You will process them immediately," she said.

"I cannot do that."

"Very well, I will inform Joseph Stalin that you cannot do it as I ask."

After moment in which the threat sank in, he said, "I will stop everything else and do it now."

"Thank you," she said.

Within an hour, with everyone else waiting, they received their passports under their married name of Krylenko. Nadya knew how to use the power of being Stalin's wife.

We meandered out to the street with Max and Eliena—delighted—looking at their passports. We found Victor parking at the curb.

Nadya, the commander in chief, turned to them and said, "Pack one suitcase each and meet us at the railroad station within two hours. Victor will take you to your apartment and then to the railroad station."

I leaned over and asked, "Victor, did you hear that?"

Victor nodded and looked straight ahead. Max opened the rear door to admit Eliena and then clambered in. Victor did not look happy.

Nadya repeated, "In two hours," and Max nodded. Victor drove away, and Nadya turned to me. "And now, my darling Philip, it will take an hour or more to walk to the railway station. A lovely day for a stroll through Moscow, my beloved Moscow. Look at the snow and frost on the trees, lacy and beautiful." Nadya took my arm and said, "Let's walk."

We walked in silence and enjoyed the cold winter sun and the beauty of the city in winter.

Then I asked, "At what frontier are we sending them out of the country?"

"Finland, Poland, Hungary, whatever," she said.

"This might be important," I said. "The clerk at the marriage bureau seemed to wonder, and the clerk at the passport office needed to be threatened before he would process it right away. If either of them decides to report this, and the report reaches Stalin, it could mean curtains for Max and Eliena."

Nadya stopped on the curb. "You may be right," she said thoughtfully.

I asked, "Where would Stalin expect them to leave the country if he found out about it?"

"Max is from the West, and Joseph would expect him to go to the nearest frontier that would take him to a Western country."

"Where would Stalin least expect him to go?"

Nadya brightened. "Siberia! Joseph was sent into exile in Siberia under the Tsar, and he hated it so much he is almost ready to give it to China."

"It takes a week to cross Siberia on the trans-Siberian railway. We are trying to get them out of the country, not lose them in it."

Nadya announced, "The railway goes straight through to Vladivostok on the Pacific coast, and there is no way they can get lost unless they get off the train. They can take a ship from there to the United States and eat oranges in California."

"That crosses six time zones and is a long, miserable trip."

She insisted, "Better a week of travel than a short trip and a bullet in the head. It's settled."

I gave Nadya's plan some thought and agreed it was the best solution.

Nadya was smiling with satisfaction at her cleverness. The brisk walk had put roses in her cheeks and sparkles in her dark eyes.

"I love you, Nadya," I heard my voice say. The confession was visceral and involuntary.

She looked up at me seriously. She kissed the fingertips of her gloved hand and placed them on my lips. "I understand how you feel. I could easily love you if I were to let it happen, but I will not. I am Stalin's wife and, no matter what kind of man he is, I am still Stalin's wife."

"Caesar's wife must be above reproach." I sighed.

She nodded. "We can be *po dusham*, heart-to-heart, and love each other in every way but one. You must learn to be *maskirovannoye*—one who masks his feelings."

I smiled wryly. "That's better than nothing."

She smiled wistfully. "You are such a decent man."

"Sounds pretty boring," I said.

"Every moment with you delights me," she said.

After an awkward moment in which we wanted to hug but could not, I said, "Let's not keep the newlyweds waiting. They are not safely out of the country yet."

Nadya took my arm, and we marched in step all the way to the railroad station without another word between us.

Max and Eliena were waiting for us, looking worried, with Victor's car standing at the curb. Relief swept over their faces when they saw us approaching.

Nadya smiled and said, "I hope you two have more than one change of underwear."

Nonplussed, Max asked, "Why?"

She said, "We are sending you through Siberia to Vladivostok, where you can get a ship to America. We began to worry that one of the clerks might get suspicious and send in a report that reaches Stalin. Siberia is the last direction he would expect you to go, and so that is where you will go. It will be long and tiring, but sometimes, the long way around is the short way home."

"Good thinking," Max said.

Nadya went to the ticket window and purchased two one-way tickets to Vladivostok. She gave the tickets to Max and said, "Let's find the best seats on the train for you." We walked to the tracks with the train scheduled to depart East and walked through car after car filled with people sprawling in pajamas and carrying enough food for a week's journey. Then we came to a car with sleeping accommodations and found a cabin that was private and empty. She then commandeered the cabin and snapped her fingers to get the porter's attention. She showed him her all-powerful party card and warned, "See to it that the Krylenkos are undisturbed in this cabin all the way to Vladivostok. If I hear that anyone has usurped this compartment, you will personally answer to me."

The porter was intimidated and bowed from the waist.

We turned to say goodbye to Max and Eliena for the last time. There were hugs and handshakes all around. These were brave, intelligent, good people we were losing. We four had become fast friends who trusted one another.

Max said, "You two have taken outrageous chances to save us."

Nadya said, "You're worth it."

Max said, sadly, "It's probably goodbye forever."

Nadya smiled. "It was a joy to know both of you."

The blast of the locomotive whistle signaled it was time to go. We walked to the exit of the car and stood on the platform, waving goodbye as the train pulled away.

Then it was done, and they were on their way. Nadya took my arm, and we walked in silence to where Victor was waiting at the curb.

Nadya frowned and said, "Bad things are going to happen when Joseph discovers that Max has vanished. He may decide to finish off Trotsky while he can still get his hands on him. Find him and warn him to get out of the Soviet Union as soon as he can, any way he can."

She offered her hand for a comradely handshake, revolutionary style, but I bowed and lifted her wrist to my lips, Tsarist style. I murmured quietly, "I cannot be *maskirovannoye* with you."

"Try harder," she said with a repressed smile.

I laughed openly, the tension gone now that Max and Eliena had safely escaped. I turned to Victor and said, "Trotsky's apartment."

18

> The best eraser is a ball of lead.
> Unwanted men and memories
> vanish with a bullet to the head
> as if they never were—
> —Joseph Stalin

I lay on my back on the straw and remembered the last dinner at the Voroshilovs. I groaned to think of how Stalin had vulgarized and brutalized Nadya in front of all the dinner guests. Unforgivable. Even the poem I wrote for her could not diminish the horror of that revelation.

Dinner at the Voroshilovs was different this time. Max was unavailable to brighten the conversation of the evening because he and Eliena had fled through Siberia to escape from Stalin's assassins and hopefully find their way to safety in America. The guests were no longer strangers but well-known to me: Beria, who had had a limousine converted to a soundproofed bedroom in the rear and cruised the streets of Moscow looking for pretty women to be seized by his driver and guards and then gang-raped and sodomized; Molotov the "stone-ass," as he was called, who would pull down his pants and sit on a block of ice if Stalin told him to do so; Dzershzinsky the Pole, who hunted down dissenters and whose pointed finger meant torture and death; Zinoviev, who preened and strutted and considered himself irresistible to women; Kamenev and Kaganovich, two Jews who had betrayed their heritage in exchange for power; Voroshilov and Ordzhonikidze, two decent men and friends of Stalin's youth who were content to be in the second or third ranks of power, and Stalin knew it; and an assortment of thugs who were loyal to Stalin because without Stalin, they were nothing.

The Kremlin wives huddled near their husbands, laughing nervously and hoping not to be noticed, trying not to say anything that would annoy Joseph Stalin. The wives lived in perpetual fear that the downfall of their husbands would mean the loss of their perquisites.

The ambiance at the Voroshilovs had also changed since the first dinner. The chitchat over vodka and nibbles were grim. The dream of Socialism in one country had been shaken by the ferocious resistance of the peasants to being forced onto collective farms. Machine guns found as much use against the Russian and Ukrainian people as they did against the Germans in the Great War. At Tambov, tanks needed to be used to crush the farmers fighting for their land and their way of life. Despite this, the peasants fought back and buried grain and slaughtered livestock in the tens of millions.

Stalin too had changed. A pattern of drinking a glass or two of vodka a day expanded to swilling a quart or more a day. The anguish of not knowing what to do was dissolved in alcohol.

When I walked into the party, resplendent in my Ukrainian embroidered tunic, I saw Nadya and Stalin talking to the Voroshilovs. Stalin was weaving a little as he stood, and I knew that he had had a few drinks before the party. This was the first time I had seen him since returning from Ukraine, and the puffiness of his face was shocking. I had asked for an interview to work on his biography, but he refused.

Nadya saw me and smiled as she hurried over to offer her cheek for a kiss. As I leaned to her face, her back to Stalin, she said through a smile, "Don't change expression as I talk to you."

I straightened up and managed to look charming. A lifetime of lies gives one *panache*.

Nadya said through a social smile, "Joseph knows that Max and Eliena have escaped, and he is furious. He knows that Trotsky has vanished, and he is ready to kill somebody. He suspects that we are lovers and says he can see the sparks whenever we are together."

I smiled and said, "That really makes my evening."

Nadya continued, "The reports from Ukraine are ghastly, and he suspects everyone of turning against him."

"I wonder why," I said, tongue in cheek.

"He has been drinking heavily, and his mood is ugly, ugly, ugly—the worst I have ever seen." Then she pirouetted, about to walk back toward Stalin, twittering over her shoulder, "Have a nice time," and fluttered her hands goodbye.

Nadya was wearing a sheath dress of satin finish that flaunted the glory of her figure.

Then I glanced up to see the malevolent stare of Stalin, looking at me as I looked at her.

Mrs. Voroshilov called the guests to dinner, and Nadya signaled for me to sit next to her and her husband.

Was this a joke? I wondered. But when I pulled out the chair next to Nadya, Stalin pointed to a place halfway down the table and said, "You sit there."

Nadya frowned with flashing eyes but did not want to make a scene, given his evil mood.

I nodded and took my place halfway down the table where he had pointed and accepted my demotion with whatever grace I could muster.

There was no hubbub of comraderie as before, no outbursts of laughter, no toasts to the future of Socialism, no bonhomie. The dinner party felt like a wake.

Mrs. Voroshilov seemed distressed. She stood up and announced with a wan smile, "We have a special treat tonight. Roast suckling pig stuffed with truffles and special sauces from France."

Stalin applauded loudly with a mocking smile, so everyone else applauded too.

When the clapping died down, Stalin leaned over the table and boomed at me, "Comrade Makharov! Tell us about your trip to the countryside. Did you and Max and Eliena and Stalin's wife enjoy yourselves?"

I stared into baleful Asiatic eyes but stood my ground. "We saw much suffering by the people, and we did not enjoy it."

Nadya flashed a good-for-you look at me.

"Much suffering, eh? Why was that?" Stalin's face was malevolent.

Something inside me refused to quail. "The peasants are fighting the attempts to take their food and force them onto collective farms. People are dying by the millions."

Stalin's face suffused red. "The deaths of all those people were due to the enthusiasm of the Red Guards to their excesses in carrying out my orders. Didn't you read my article, 'Dizzy with Success,' explaining it all?"

Nadya snapped, "Max Eastman's article explained it better."

Stalin ignored her and bored into me. "Why don't you give us your version? We are all ears."

I could see that Stalin had decided to skewer me before the others and to humiliate me before Nadya. I took my life in my hands. "Red Guards are machine-gunning whole families to take what they have and force them onto collective farms."

"For their own good!" Stalin barked.

"What good is it to be killed?" I said, determined not to lie or curry favor.

A stunned silence fell over the guests, and everyone yearned to be anywhere but here.

Nadya saw what was coming and turned to Stalin. "Joseph, are you so blind with ambition that you cannot see the consequences of what you are doing? People are starving to death by the millions because of your policies." Her voice became shrill. "Mothers are eating the bodies of their own dead children! I saw it with my own eyes!"

Stalin rumbled boozily, "What you are talking about is 'subjective reality.' 'Objective reality' is that we are building Socialism for the happiness of mankind, and if we have to kill a few cockroaches along the way, it's a small price to pay in the grand scheme of things."

Nadya shrilled, "Killing cockroaches is what Peter the Great called killing innocent people!"

Stalin picked up a tumbler of vodka and drank it straight down. "You think small," he said.

Nadya turned in her chair to face him. "You are imposing hell on people in the name of mankind."

Stalin scoffed, "Peasants are not really people. They are little more than livestock."

"When did you ever step down from your throne of books and politics to talk to the people whose lives you are destroying?"

"I don't need to talk to them to know what is good for them," Stalin mumbled thickly. "Objective reality is found in the writings of Marx, Engels, and Lenin. Objective reality—the greater good for mankind—is all that matters in planning policies for the new Socialist order."

Nadya shouted, "Objective reality! Subjective reality! The only reality is your own ambition! You want to throw a giant shadow across Russia—across the world—that eclipses the dreams of Peter the Great and Ivan the Terrible! You built the mausoleum of Lenin for no better reason than to stand on it as a pedestal for your own glory!"

A gasp of horror rippled through the guests, and they sat hypnotized, as if watching a tragedy.

Nadya ranted, "In the name of peace, justice, and the brotherhood of man, you kill and kill and kill! You are consumed with lust for greatness and are building it on the bones of dead and dying people. You are a monster!"

Dead silence. I watched with the others and wondered what the end to this would be.

Stalin rose to his feet with his face livid and turned to her. He pointed to me and said, "How dare you talk to me like that when Makharov has been plowing your *pizda*. You *blyad!*"

Nadya leaped to her feet and faced him. "How dare you call me a whore! I have never betrayed you with another man. Not once!"

Stalin pointed again at me. "Don't tell me that your nights in Ukraine were not spent *pishol v pizdu* with Philip Makharov."

"I was Stalin's wife during every minute of the trip, and Philip was a perfect gentleman."

"You mean he was gentle with his *khuy*, as you like it."

Nadya exploded into fury and slapped his face with a loud *whack!*

Stalin grabbed Nadya by the throat and sank in his thumbs and shook her violently. She writhed and struggled and strangled. Men leaped up but held back, afraid to touch Stalin.

I was on my feet and halfway there when she rolled her eyes toward me for help. I grabbed Stalin's wrists and tried to pull them loose from the throat of Nadya, who was nearly unconscious, but I could not break his maniacal hold. The hands of a giant were throttling a butterfly. In desperation, I cocked my fist, and with all the strength I could muster—from the floor up—I smashed Joseph Stalin in the mouth.

Stalin let go and staggered back, his rage broken, blood streaming from his mouth.

Nadya sank choking and coughing to her chair.

Stalin turned to face me, and I knew I was a dead man. He touched his bloody mouth and looked down at the blood on his fingers. He said, "I thought you were a coward."

"I am a coward."

"I don't think so," he said with grudging respect. "Nor does she."

Stalin looked down at Nadya, who was trembling from head to toe. He said, "I want the hero of the evening to escort Stalin's wife home. I know she will be safe in your care because you are willing to die for her."

Nadya murmured, "No. I want to go home with my husband."

Stalin flared again, "Your husband orders you to go home with your lover."

Nadya looked up with flashing dark eyes. She stood up and faced him. "I don't have a lover. And I do not take orders from a bullying husband!"

"No?" he snarled, very drunk. "You will take orders from your father! Your father orders you to go home with Philip Makharov!"

"My father?" she gasped. "*You* are my father! And *you* are the father of Vassily and Svetlana? Have I been making love all these years with my own father?" She stood for a long moment, then wailed in horror, "I am the daughter of Joseph Stalin!"

Stalin stopped in shock at what he had said. He looked about at the stunned guests. Angrily he yelled, "Look what you have made me say! Now everybody knows!"

Anguish spread over Nadya's face, and tears filled her eyes. "The poems you wrote. The love poems you wrote?"

Stalin shouted, "I wrote those for your mother, Olga, who I loved more than life itself. Dead as she is, she means more to me than you ever have or ever could. She and I are one—now and forever—and you are only a woman I use *ebat* because you look like her."

Nadya sank to her chair again and began to weep convulsively into her hands.

I heard the sound of my voice saying, "You brutal bastard! How could you say that to her?"

I found myself cocking my fist and swinging again until my arms were grabbed and stopped by the other men. I struggled like a wild man to hit Stalin again.

Stalin stood before me until I calmed down. "Brave men are dangerous," he said.

Nadya announced, "Brave women are dangerous." She suddenly rose to her feet in full possession of herself and stared at Stalin with the eyes of a raptor. She turned to me and said, "My father wants me to leave the party and go home with you. We both want you to take me home because we both know I am safe with Philip Makharov."

Stalin gestured for the men to let go of my arms. "Take her home," he said. "I will deal with each of you later."

The composure of Nadya was astonishing. She had just been stripped of every remaining illusion and belief—shattered emotionally—yet there she was, pulled together. She turned her luminous dark eyes to me, took my arm, and said, "Have Victor drive me home. We will leave the limousine for my father."

"Of course," I said and nodded politely to Joseph Stalin. I was as good as dead, but I wanted Nadya to be proud of me. She had turned to me as the man who loved her, for protection, and I was calm about paying the price. We made a regal pair as we walked the length of the dining room before the giants of the new Soviet Union, all those who were trampling the past and hammering out the new Socialist order. I saw respect in their eyes, a new experience for me. We were given our coats and matter-of-factly put them on.

We stepped out into bitter cold, and as soon as she was out of sight of the others, she broke down again.

"All of those poems, all of those beautiful poems…were written for my mother." She wept.

For a long moment, I did not know what to do. Then I remembered the paper in my pocket. I took it out and unfolded it. I said, "This poem was written for you. There is no rhyme or meter to it because I don't know how to do that. But it's from the heart."

Surprised, she took it to read, but the light was very bad. There was a street lamp farther down the street, and we walked over to it.

Victor pulled up to the curb to wait with the motor running, but I gestured for him to park farther down the street. He nodded and parked a short distance away.

The wind suddenly tore at the paper, but Nadya grabbed it with both hands and then began to read it silently:

Nadya

How can I not think of you when the first glimmer of dawn heralds another day with the image of your face before my unopened eyes?

How can I not be with you when every waking hour is consumed with longing for your lovely presence awaiting the touch of a kiss?

How can I not worship you when your being and forms give shape to my dreams of a perfect woman in love and awakened by desire?

How can I not be part of you when the closeness we share embraces every plane of human experience to fuse you with me as one?

Philip Makharov

"Did you really write this for me?" she said, looking up with ineffable sweetness.

"I wrote it for you." I smiled.

"It's beautiful. Thank you so much, Philip." She folded it up and looked at it in her hand. "The poem has only one error—there is one plane of experience we have not shared."

I took her by the hand. "It's time to go home." We walked together to the car, and I told Victor, "Drive us to Comrade Nadya's residence." He nodded and restarted the car engine.

I opened the rear door for Nadya and clambered in after her. We covered our laps with a lap blanket. Nadya sat staring at the poem, then opened and reread it as the car pulled away from the curb. She turned and stared at me strangely for a long moment with different eyes, then she leaned forward to tap Victor on the shoulder and shout over the clatter of the engine, "Drive us first to Comrade Makharov's residence."

"But why?" I asked.

Nadya turned to me and mouthed the words, "I love you." Then she leaned over to whisper, behind a cupped hand, "As I said, there is one plane of human experience you and I have not shared so far. I want to know the love of a man I love who is not my father—you."

I was stunned by the implications and knew that I would have to say no to another man's wife but did not know how without insulting her. As we rode, looking straight ahead as passengers, Nadya's hand slid under the lap blanket and found its way over to me and then rested on my *khuy*. She began to quietly stroke and fondle it, looking impassively straight ahead, and by the time we reached my apartment, saying no was out of the question.

I opened the car door, grateful for the covering greatcoat, and took Nadya's hand to help her out. Nadya turned to Victor and said imperiously, "You will wait here until I return." She turned and walked elegantly toward the front door, and I began to follow after.

Victor called out anxiously, "Comrade Makharov," and gestured for me to come back. I returned and leaned over to hear him say, "No, comrade. Not with Stalin's wife. *Prosim!*"

"Thank you, my friend," I said. "But this is my life—or what's left of it after tonight."

Victor bowed his head and put his hand to his face.

I joined Nadya at the front door, unlocked it, and we walked together to the apartment door. I opened it and let her into the darkened room. As usual, the power was out, and electric lights useless, I had candles placed all around the apartment and knew where they were. One by one, I lit matches and groped around lighting candles from room to room, in the bedroom, the bathroom, and the study, feeling guilty that she was still another man's wife.

When I returned, I was startled to find Nadya standing naked. She had quietly stripped to the flesh and revealed the most finely made woman I had ever seen. Nadya had full but upright breasts that denied she had ever been a mother, a tiny waist that swelled to delicate hips, down to womanly thighs with straight legs and dainty feet. She was erotic perfection, yet I hesitated.

"You are still Stalin's wife," I said.

"I am Stalin's daughter—and never was his wife. Joseph's marriage to me was illegal incest. No culture in the world permits a father to marry his own daughter. And when it happens and becomes known, the marriage is instantly cancelled as if it never occurred. Joseph is not my husband, and I am not—and never have been—Stalin's wife."

Nadya misread my silence and was suddenly afraid that having offered herself to me, naked, she would suffer the humiliation of rejection. She begged, offering her hands, "Could you love the used, betrayed, violated daughter of Joseph Stalin?"

"I would marry you this minute and love your children as my own." I meant it.

Joy and relief swept over her face, and she closed her eyes for a moment to savor my words. Then she came forward with shining eyes and serene confidence and began to remove my clothing, article by article, kissing and caressing me as she did so. She took me by the hand and walked me to the bed, pulled back the cover, and, with impish eyes and bitch-goddess smile, leaned over to peer studiously at my *khuy*. She giggled and said, "If that is really 'all you,' I will certainly marry you."

We laughed together as one, and I fell into bed. She followed me under the covers and kissed me on the lips. Then we loved.

TO SOME ABSENT GOD

During the following hours, I exhausted myself in Nadya. Each time, I thought it would be the last time, but the sight of her, the scent of rose petals, the feel of her skin and body, the press of her mouth, and the touch of her fingers aroused me again and again.

Eventually I was drained and needed a respite. We lay there holding hands and spinning dreams until I made the mistake of closing my eyes for an instant. When I opened them again, it was daylight, and Nadezhda Sergeevna Alliluyeva was gone.

A note on her pillow read as follows:

> Dearest Philip,
>
> I love you for really being all the good things
> I believed you were.
>
> Nadya

19

> Happiness is this:
> Pick the time of your enemy's death,
> kill him slowly and watch his last breath,
> then retire to slumber in bliss.
>
> —Joseph Stalin

Nadya is *dead!* The words tore through me like an iron beak slashing through my breastbone to tear out my heart! The anguish was unbearable, and I did not care whether I lived or died as the Red Guards dragged me out of the apartment and down to the waiting police van. I yelled, "No! No! No! No!" all the way in denial of her death, resisting her end with every fiber of my being. It could not be that warm, loving Nadya was dead! It could not be she was a corpse!

The biggest of the two Red Guards stopped and punched me in the stomach to shut me up. I doubled to the sidewalk, choking and gasping. The blow was followed by the stench of garlic breath as he leaned down and snarled, "She shot herself."

A suicide—like her mother!

The big hoglike guard rumbled to the other, "Get the box of papers about Stalin's biography." The smaller guard squeaked yes and ran into the apartment and returned carrying the box in his arms.

The Hog handcuffed my wrists, saying, "Stalin wants to know what you have been writing about him." I was shoved into the caged vehicle and driven to Lubianka prison to be thrown into a cell stinking with dank smells and alive with cockroaches.

My head was swimming. I had to know how, why, where she had died. I hoped desperately that this was a cruel hoax by Stalin to make me suffer for loving her. He was a diabolical bastard, and I would not put it past him. I yearned to see Nadya appear outside the cell door and command, "Stalin's wife orders you to release Philip Makharov this instant." I longed to be with her on any terms, if only she was still alive. I sat on the bunk and wept uncontrollably—like a child—and could think only of Nadya. What happened to me now did not matter.

The huge guard I now thought of as "Hog" stopped and watched me but said nothing. I sensed there was something decent about him but did not care as I wallowed in misery. Hog put bread and cabbage soup in at mealtimes and took away the piss bucket without saying anything. I lay on the bench, and my head throbbed with the litany, "Nadya is dead! Nadya is dead! Nadya is dead!"

Hog announced, "You have a visitor."

I sat up in a wild, crazy, desperate hope of seeing Nadya standing there, but it was Victor. He stood there solemnly holding a package in his hands.

Hog ordered, "Open the package."

Victor did as he was told, and Hog rummaged through cold chicken, bread, apples, and a small bottle of vodka.

Victor said, "No files or weapons... Could we have two cups?"

Hog thought for a moment and asked, "You two are old comrades?"

Victor nodded. "We are old comrades."

Hog left and returned with two small glasses, then unlocked the cell door to admit Victor, and locked it afterward. He looked at us through the bars, facing each other in silence, then said, "I have to take a shit. Will you two be all right in there for a while?"

We nodded appreciatively. Hog was giving us private time to talk while he left.

As Victor unscrewed the bottle and poured up two glasses of vodka, I asked, "Is Nadya really dead?"

Victor handed me a glass, then lifted his own, and said, "To the soul of Nadezhda Sergeevna Alliluyeva."

It was true. Nadya was dead. We clinked glasses and tossed down the vodka neat for the quickest possible effect, a blessing when it came.

A thought crossed my mind. "Does Stalin know you have come to see me?"

"Yes," Victor said. "I have worked for Joseph Stalin from the very beginning. I told him how often you had shared what you had with me, and I wanted to repay your kindness."

I gasped. "Have you been informing on me to Stalin…about everything?"

"Almost everything. I did not tell him of your tryst with Comrade Nadya, your trips to see Trotsky, or your actions in putting Max Eastman and Eliena Krylenko on the train to Siberia."

I almost laughed. "You are a terrible agent for Stalin."

"I hope so," he said. "One must be human."

Victor looked me in the eyes and said, "You will want to know what happened to her," he said, putting down his glass and gathering his thoughts.

"Yes," I said.

"When she came out of your apartment, I drove her to their residence in the Kremlin. Stalin had not yet returned from the party at the Voroshilovs."

"We were together for hours," I said. "How could she have returned first?"

"You two left the party very early, and the party ended very, very late. Stalin stumbled in just before dawn in a raging temper, storming and yelling for his wife. There was a loud argument and then a pistol shot. Stalin's driver ran into the apartment and saw Nadya lying face-down, shot in the back."

"Then it was murder," I said.

Victor nodded. "It is difficult to commit suicide by shooting oneself in the back."

"Stalin will pay for that," I gloated.

"No. He will not," Victor retorted. "It has been announced by the Kremlin that she committed suicide, and Stalin has forbidden any autopsy."

"He can't get away with that," I flared.

"Yes, he can," Victor insisted. "And if you say anything or I say anything, it will mean a bullet in the head and an unmarked grave for each of us."

I did not care, but I nodded.

Hog came back and said, with a hint of a smile, "Time is up."

Victor stood up and offered me his hand, saying, "Goodbye, Comrade Makharov. I do not believe we will meet again." We shook hands, and I clapped him on the shoulder. Hog unlocked the door and let Victor out of the cell. Victor gave me a last smile and wave outside the bars and then departed.

When Hog returned to stand guard, I divided the last of the vodka between the two cups. I handed one through the bars to him and said, "Comrades should share."

Hog took the glass and tossed the vodka down, neat. He handed back the glass and, without a word, walked away. Then I sat down to eat the chicken, bread, and apples, the first decent meal I had had since being arrested. I noticed something slender and wrapped in paper. I opened it to find four wood matches and a cigar—a Cuban cigar. Victor had saved one for me. I smiled and ran it under my nose to savor the fragrance. I did not have the heart to light it in the gloom of Nadya's death and put it in my shirt for another time, if there was another time.

The next day, Hog and Squeaky appeared outside my cell. Hog said, "Comrade Stalin has ordered that you be brought to him."

It was a relief. Anything to break the grimness of stone walls and the pain of losing Nadya. The cell door was opened, and I was marched down a corridor to what I thought would be an interrogation room. Partly, I was apprehensive, and mostly, I just did not give a damn. Stalin could *v-rot-yebis*. To my surprise, Hog put a cap on my head and a greatcoat on my shoulders and walked me out to where Stalin's limousine waited at the curb. Hog opened the door so I could enter and sit in the center, then he and Squeaky sat on either side. Without a word, the driver drove the limousine toward the Kremlin.

I was surprised but accepted whatever would come. And I savored the ambiance of Moscow, the Moscow that Nadya and I had walked through, loving it: wide thoroughfares, parks, and busy people bundled to the eyes to keep out the cold. A light snow had fallen and transformed the images of everything: the mounds of dirty snow had been coated in white to create a lumpy fairyland, and the snow on tree branches and twigs had left a tracery that gave the appearance of fine lace hung before massive gray buildings. Even the sun peeked out, a rare thing in winter, to render everything in silverpoint etching. My heart lifted, and I was glad to see again what Nadya and I had shared in our walk to the railroad station.

Then we approached the gloomy Kremlin walls, and everything changed. Red Guards were everywhere carrying rifles and pistols. Anyone who came here without authorization would face overwhelming force. The driver parked the limousine. We clambered out of the automobile, and I was marched into a drab building, up a flight of stairs, and down a darkened corridor to Stalin's office. Hog knocked on the door and was answered by a voice saying, "Come in." We entered to find Joseph Stalin, formidable as ever, seated behind a huge desk.

He stood up and walked around it and ordered Hog and Squeaky, "Hold his arms."

They did so. Then Stalin clenched his fist and, with all his power, smashed me in the mouth. The blow knocked me over backward, and only the hold of the guards kept me from falling. I felt my lips had split, pieces of teeth were floating around, and my mouth was filling up with blood that spilled out and ran off my chin.

Stalin barked, "That's for hitting me at the Voroshilovs." Then he said, "Let him go."

I weaved as I stood, my mind reeling.

"Take this," he said, pulling a handkerchief from his pocket and handing it to me.

I mopped blood from my mouth and chin, spit pieces into the handkerchief, and waited for whatever might come.

Stalin ordered the guards, "Pull up two chairs for us."

They dragged two chairs over in front of the desk, facing each other.

Stalin said, "Wait outside."

Hog and Squeaky walked quietly out and closed the door behind them.

Stalin waved toward a chair, and I sat down. He walked over to a table lined with liquor bottles and glasses. He poured an amber-colored fluid into two glasses, then walked back and handed one to me. "American vodka. They call it whiskey. It will kill the pain of anything."

I sipped a little whiskey, and it burned my smashed lips.

Stalin sat down in the facing chair and leaned forward to look intently at me.

I was surprised to see them red and swollen. The man of steel had been weeping.

Stalin raised his glass and said, "To the good *pizda* of Nadya Sergeevna."

I flared at his vulgarity to her and raised my glass to say, "The good days at Zubalovo."

Stalin shook suddenly, as if slapped on the back, and murmured, "The good days at Zubalovo."

We downed the whiskey and, for a long moment, stared at each other, each held by the memory of Nadya.

"My grief is twice yours," Stalin murmured. "She was my daughter as well as my wife, and my suffering is doubled."

I said nothing as I stared at the murderer.

Stalin brightened a little as he stared into memory. "When Nadya was two years old, she fell into the water at Baku. I jumped into a stormy sea to save her… I saved Nadya's life then." Moisture rimmed his eyes for a moment, then he pulled himself together.

At last, Stalin said, "How often did you go to bed with Stalin's wife?"

"I never had sex with Stalin's wife," I said, and I thought, *Only his daughter.*

Stalin angrily smashed me in the cheek from where he sat, rocking me straight back in the chair. He shouted, "Do you think I am a fool? Do you think I could not see the sparks flying between you? All those nights in Ukraine away from my eyes! Tell me the truth!"

"The truth is that I never had sex with Stalin's wife," I said stubbornly, clinging to the distinction as my eye began to swell and close. "Nadya was faithful to you for as long as she was Stalin's wife."

"So?" he said, taking a folded piece of paper from his pocket and unfolding it. He held the poem I had written for Nadya before my face. "What is this if not a love poem?"

"You broke Nadya's heart by never writing a love poem for her after writing so many for another woman. I did not want to see her hurt. I wrote the poem so she would have at least one poem written by a man who loved her. And yes, I did love her. But I never had sex with Stalin's wife."

Stalin bowed his head. "How could I write love poems to my own daughter? I knew the truth, and she did not. It was Nadya who first seduced me when she was little more than a child. I knew I should have said no, but I didn't. And every time after that, it became harder to say that this is wrong because I am your father. The right time, place, and circumstance never happened. Once we had our first child, it became impossible to tell Nadya that she had had a baby by her own father." His eyes welled with tears. He stood up and turned away to the desk to lean on it with his hands. He murmured, "What have I done?" Stalin took as much time as he needed to regain his composure. When he turned around and sat down, he was once again himself, a man of steel. He said, "Do you want to visit her grave at Novo-Devichy?"

I snapped, "Nadya wanted to be buried among the birches of Zubalovo."

"Important people are buried at Novo-Devichy," he murmured, surprised.

"There is no status among the dead. There is only honoring their wishes after they are gone."

"Do you want to see her grave?"

"No. I want to remember her alive."

Stalin thought for a moment and asked, "What will I do with you? I believe that you loved her but did not have sex with Stalin's wife. And I have done unforgivable things to Nadya. Yet I cannot turn you loose in Russia to tell and write what you know of Nadya and me. I have read enough of your biography of me to know that your viewpoint is not what I want posterity to read, and I have had all of it burned."

I shrugged. I knew that the truth would not be published in Stalin's Soviet Union.

Stalin inquired, "Are you willing to begin again and write it as I tell you?"

"I won't lie for you," I said, my left eye now swollen shut.

"You have balls, Makharov," he said. "I'll give you that. You have balls."

I shrugged. Who cares about macho posturing at a time like this?

Stalin stared long and hard at me. "Did you really love my daughter?"

"I loved her," I said as clearly as I could manage through a mashed mouth.

"Would you have married her, if you could?"

"I'd have married her in a minute, for a lifetime."

Stalin's head bowed, and he seemed to be looking at his boots. Then he looked up with the vulnerability of a child. "How much better things would have turned out if you could have married Nadya when she came of age. Vassily and Svetlana would then have been my grandchildren instead of my children. As lovely as she was, I felt ashamed to make love with her. She sensed my reserve and believed there was something unattractive about her. The problem was not in her but in me. You would have been right for her. And for what it is worth, I might have liked having brave and intelligent Philip Makharov as a son-in-law."

That comment popped open even my swollen eye.

Stalin picked up the poem from the desk and said, "I will have this interred in a capsule at her grave, so she will have one poem written by a man who loved her."

"Thank you."

Then Stalin said, "I will not have you executed on one condition—your sworn promise that you will not talk or write about Stalin's wife or me. I will deport you, but you will live."

"I will not talk or write about you or Nadya, wherever I am," I said, but I lied.

"Then you will cross the border at Belo-Ostrov and walk into Finland a free man. Remember, if you keep your word, I will keep mine. I give you your life in memory of Nadya Sergeevna Alliluyeva, whom, it is fair to say, we both loved."

20

For Olga

> We cannot remember what we feel,
> but only recall what happened.
> Let me be glad to steal
> fire from the loving past
> and read in burning verse
> the passion that once was real.
>
> —Joseph Stalin

"Belo-Ostrov! Belo-Ostrov!" I heard in the distance. I watched Hog leaning out the opening of the door and looking ahead down the track. I had to wonder if it was the beginning or the end for me.

Hog turned back to me, smiled, and went over to his rucksack to pull out a quart of vodka—a quart—and a large package. He sat before me and placed them between us and signaled for Squeaky to join us. Hog took out three nesting cups, set them up, and poured them full of vodka. They slopped a little in the rocking of the railroad car that had become home. Then he opened the package to reveal *kasha,* dried fish, boiled beef, sliced ham, a jar of mustard, and jar of horseradish sauce—a farewell feast of mouthwatering proportions.

Hog raised his cup and said, "To good comrades."

Squeaky and I smiled as we raised our cups to say, "Comrades!"

Then we ate and drank, and the meal was delicious. Not in the same class as dinner at the Voroshilovs, but delicious all the same. For a long while, we ate in silence. Every time my cup was empty, Hog refilled it, and I began to be a bit light-headed. But what the hell, consider it a celebration that I had made it this far.

I murmured, "One must live a little."

"What did you say?" Hog asked with a smile.

"I am just talking to my vodka."

"Talk to us instead," Hog said.

"About what?"

"About your writing and what you plan to do as a free man. I read some pages in Stalin's biography, and you write extremely well. Your prose is poetry."

Surprised, I asked, "Where did you learn to read?"

Hog replied, "My father was a teacher in a village in Siberia."

I looked at Squeaky. "Can you read too?"

He shook his head no and said, "He reads to me."

Suddenly, the two rough and smelly guards had faces, minds, and souls. They were people.

"Well," I said, downing a cup of vodka, "how much of Stalin's biography did you read?"

Hog grinned. "More than Stalin did. It will never be published. Your analysis of Joseph Stalin made me wonder why you were not shot on the spot. Especially," he added, "since you were obviously in love with Stalin's wife."

"Obviously?"

"Obviously... Well," Hog said, "what are you going to write about?"

"My experiences in the revolution, I suppose. There is a lot of interest abroad in what is going on in the Soviet Union."

"Will those experiences include Stalin's wife?" Hog asked quietly.

"Of course. She was a wonderful human being. I will write what I know and feel about her." How could I not write about Joseph Stalin and Nadya, a story worthy of Greek tragedy. As Lenin said, "Promises are like pie crusts—made to be broken."

Hog changed the subject, saying, "Let's finish the meal with a special treat before we pull into Belo-Ostrov." He rolled over to his rucksack and pulled out something wrapped in paper. He unrolled it to reveal three cigars, one of which he handed to me.

I smelled its fragrance and recognized it immediately. I said, "This is a very fine cigar—where did you get it?"

"We were sent to arrest Leon Trotsky, but he and his wife disappeared from their apartment even though agents watched him all the time. He left behind a box of Cuban cigars."

I smiled inwardly, remembering Trotsky's escape route.

I asked, "Where is Trotsky now?"

"I was told in Prinkipo, but on his way to Mexico."

"Out of Stalin's reach?"

"Nobody is out of Stalin's reach."

Then I remembered the American. "Do you know what became of Max Eastman and Eliena Krylenko?"

Hog said, "I heard that they fled East on the trans-Siberian railway for Vladivostok but got off the train halfway and headed south to India. I heard they crossed the Himalayas on the backs of yaks and took a ship from Calcutta to New York."

"Why didn't they go all the way to Vladivostok?"

"Someone sent them a cable saying that a welcoming committee was waiting for them."

"Who sent the cable?" I asked.

"Who knows? Comrade Stalin went into a rage when he found out. He was kicking wastebaskets and throwing ashtrays."

I knew what happened. Only Nadya would be in a position to know what Stalin was doing, especially since he did not realize that it was she who had sent Max and Eliena to safety. She probably found out what was happening and sent the cable to save them from the welcoming committee. She was sassy enough to do that. The thought of Nadya raised tears to my eyes, and I was afraid I might become a weeping drunk. How I loved her.

The locomotive began to brake and slow down with muffled crashes as each railroad car was slowed by impact with the preceding car.

Hog leaped to his feet with surprising agility, considering how much he had drunk, and went to look out the door. "We are almost there," he said.

The train slowed to the station of the Finland border, Belo-Ostrov, and the locomotive was hissing steam as it arrived.

Hog and Squeaky picked up their rifles and rucksacks and jumped to the platform while the train was still moving, and I stepped off after them but weaving a little from the effects of vodka. We walked to where a Soviet border guard stood in a kiosk checking the passports of people standing in a long line. Hog walked to the head of the line and presented a letter.

The border guard's eye popped open when he saw the signature of Joseph Stalin. He bowed deeply to Hog and to me as I crossed the border into Finland—a free man as Stalin had promised.

Hog smiled and took my notepad and pencils out of his rucksack and handed them to me across the border. He said, "A writer must have his materials."

I was almost moved to tears. I shook hands with each of them and walked woozily into Finland, quite drunk, not knowing where to turn but enormously relieved to be free at last. My writer's mind began to churn immediately. Should the book about Stalin and Nadya be a history book? I know how to write a tome of history bristling with all the verbal hardware of scholarly work, complete with footnotes and bibliography. A historical study, however, would reduce Nadya to a footnote. Joseph Stalin was such a giant that he would eclipse her as he eclipsed others in his drive to become the greatest leader in Russian history. Writing a historically accurate novel might be a better approach, but it would be a first novel for me, and I wanted to do justice to the story. Above all, I wanted to do justice to Nadya, and the format would have to serve that end. I would work it out.

Soon my mind was full of her: warm and willowy, with limpid dark eyes and throaty laugh. How she had danced like a swan at Zubalovo. I did not dare to remember our lovemaking for fear of breaking down in tears.

"Comrade Makharov!" a voice shouted from across the border. "You broke your promise not to write about Stalin's wife."

I turned just in time to see Hog and Squeak fire their rifles.

The bullets whistled by on either side of my head. I shouted, "Why did you miss?"

Hog grinned and shouted back, "Only bad writers deserve to be shot."

We all guffawed.

Then Hog said, "Good luck with writing Stalin's wife."

I opened my notebook and wrote across the top of the first page, "Stalin's Wife." I held up the notebook and showed them the page.

"A good start," Hog yelled. "Now put a book behind it."

"I promise," I said, and did not lie.

The End

About the Author

Roy Paul Madsen, PhD is recognized for his expertise and writing on film subjects. His previous books include *Animated Film, The Impact of Film,* and *Working Cinema*. His recognition for these books led to a United States Information Agency-sponsored speaking tour, during which he lectured on film topics in twenty-four countries and forty-one cities in Europe, the Middle East, and Asia. In addition to his literary achievements, Dr. Madsen is a nationally recognized painter and sculptor. His paintings were displayed and sold in the Grand Central Galleries of New York as well as other prominent galleries throughout the United States. He is a member of the prestigious National Sculpture Society, and his sculptures have been featured in galleries all over the United States. He was listed in *Who's Who in America* for six years in a row and was listed in *Who's Who in the World* in 2016. Dr. Madsen is a professor emeritus retired from San Diego State University. He lives in San Diego, California, with Barbara, his wife of many years.